"Weddings are

Nate laughed hear[…] much chatter and music echo[…] that he knew only Alice would hear. "Oh, the irony," he said.

Alice's cheeks colored deeper, and he felt a tiny stab of guilt for being so harsh. "It's not as ironic as you think," she protested. "I guess you could consider it a way to atone for what—"

"For what you did," he said bitterly.

Alice shook her head. "For what I didn't do."

Nate wished he was anywhere else. He'd often wondered what he would say if he ever saw Alice again. There was no worse time and place than right here and now.

He just had to ask one question.

"Have you ever wondered what would have happened if you hadn't walked out on our wedding?"

Alice's shoulders dropped and she looked at the floor. "Every day for the last five years."

Dear Reader,

Thank you for reading *Back to the Lake Breeze Hotel* and visiting Starlight Point. This is the fifth book of Starlight Point Stories, which also includes *Under the Boardwalk*, *Carousel Nights*, *Meet Me on the Midway* and *Until the Ride Stops*. From the first book, one of my favorite characters has been Virginia Hamilton. When her husband suddenly passes away at the beginning of the summer amusement park season, she has to be strong and make quick decisions in the best interests of her beloved Starlight Point and her three children. I'm so glad Virginia has her second chance at love five seasons later. I also love the second-chance theme of Alice and Nate meeting again after she left him at the altar five years ago. A lot can change in five years!

Writing the Starlight Point series has been an absolute joy for me, and I feel so attached to these characters and Starlight Point that I hate to let them go! I hope you'll love this book. You can stay in touch with me at amiedenman.com, follow me on Twitter, @amiedenman, or send me an email at author@amiedenman.com.

Best wishes!

Amie Denman

HEARTWARMING

Back to the Lake Breeze Hotel

——

Amie Denman

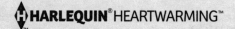

H HARLEQUIN® HEARTWARMING™

Recycling programs
for this product may
not exist in your area.

ISBN-13: 978-1-335-63354-5

Back to the Lake Breeze Hotel

Copyright © 2018 by Amie Denman

Printed in U.S.A.

Amie Denman is the author of more than a dozen contemporary romances full of humor and heart. A devoted traveler who grew up with parents who always kept a suitcase packed, she loves reading and writing books you could take on vacation. Amie believes everything is fun, especially wedding cake, show tunes, roller coasters and falling in love.

Books by Amie Denman

Harlequin Heartwarming

Starlight Point Stories

Under the Boardwalk
Carousel Nights
Meet Me on the Midway
Until the Ride Stops

Carina Press

Her Lucky Catch

Visit the Author Profile page
at Harlequin.com for more titles.

To my wonderful friends of twenty-five years,
Fran, Chris and Connie. Fran gave me
the idea for this book, but you are all an
inspiration to me! Thank you for
your loyalty, laughter and love.

CHAPTER ONE

IF ALICE BIRMINGHAM COULD HAVE custom-ordered weather, she would have requested exactly what she saw. Blue sky, temperature in the mid-seventies zone of perfection, a tiny breeze off the lake.

Planning an outdoor wedding at the end of August in Michigan was tempting fate because of late summer storms, but this ceremony was going to be all right. Alice brushed back a long strand of red hair and relaxed her shoulders.

"Are all the weddings you plan this perfect?" June Hamilton whispered, pausing to stand with Alice well behind the last row of seated guests. "I hope no one will mind if I stop and watch."

Alice smiled. "You own one third of Starlight Point. I don't think anyone is going to complain."

White chairs gleamed in neat rows on the

boardwalk. A flowered arch stretched gracefully over the heads of the groom, in a black tuxedo, and the bride, in an airy white gown. The top layer of organza on the bride's skirt caught the breeze and floated for a moment. "I should have had you plan mine and Mel's."

Alice laughed softly and whispered, "You've been married several years, right?"

June nodded. "Almost three. And I still think his annoying habits are cute. Of course, I knew all his habits long before we got married because we met when I was four."

"That's a long engagement."

"More like a long estrangement between meeting and getting married, but Starlight Point brought us back together."

Growing up in nearby Bayside, Alice was well aware of the amusement park's reputation for thrills of all kinds. With roller coasters piercing the sky, Lake Huron lapping at three sides of the peninsula, and good food and fun all summer long, Starlight Point was where everyone went to have a good time.

"You missed the best part," Alice whispered to June as they stood side by side in the August sunshine. "The moment when the bride and groom first see each other and the groom looks as if he's been hit by lightning."

"In a good way, right?"

"Yes, if the wedding is meant to be. Now that overseeing weddings is in my job description, I've developed a system for determining if the marriages will last."

June laughed quietly. "I know you're organized, but doing a spreadsheet on the couple's chances makes you sound like a bookie."

"No spreadsheets, just anecdotal observation. A thunderstruck look on the groom's face says a lot."

"The silly, slack-muscled look of love," June said. "We used to call that wonder-eyes when I was younger and worked here for the summer. All those summer romances…"

Alice knew many local kids who'd worked here for the summer and met friends and future spouses. She'd worked as a midway sweeper the summer she was seventeen. With a short broom and dustpan, she'd walked a dozen miles every day. It was tough on her feet and even worse for her fair skin, but she'd fallen in love with the amusement park.

Starlight Point had only changed a little in the past eight years. The Sea Devil ride and last year's double coaster were new additions, but there'd been some losses, too.

She remembered seeing June's father, Ford, walking the midway and greeting guests during her summer sweeping. The owner of Starlight Point had passed away about five years ago, a summer Alice would never forget for her own reasons.

"I love weddings," June whispered to Alice as they watched the exchange of vows and rings from a distance. "All that sparkle, fancy dresses, dancing and cake."

"It's intoxicating," Alice agreed. "But don't you wonder what they think the next day when they wake up?"

"I hope they eat leftover wedding cake in bed," June said. She sighed. "People should get married on this beach every day."

"As your events planner, that would be totally fine with me. We could recruit engaged couples from all over Michigan and fly them in to get married right here for one substantial fee. I could write it up for the website—white sand beach, historic hotel, on-site wedding cake baker."

"Augusta would love that," June said, referring to her sister-in-law. Gus ran three bakeries at Starlight Point, serving up cookies and doughnuts to park patrons, and a flagship bakery in downtown Bayside that turned out gorgeous wedding cakes. "Not that she needs any more business."

Alice did the mental math. She had already scheduled a wedding for almost every weekend through New Year's Eve. It wasn't what she'd signed on for when she landed the job of special events coordinator at Starlight Point, but if she had to embrace all the emotional and financial entanglements of weddings to keep her dream job, she'd keep her opinions to herself.

Mostly.

"And they walk down the aisle and boom, married perfection," Alice whispered as the bride and groom kissed to the sound of applause and the five-piece orchestra burst into a wedding exit march.

"You have to love this," June said.

"When I see the revenue coming in, I do. But now it's showtime part two with the custom-ordered dream reception coming up. Have you seen the decorations in the rotunda?"

"No," June said, "but judging from the

gleam in your eye, I'm probably going to want to get divorced just so I can get married again."

Alice chuckled. "I wouldn't advise throwing away a good man when you've got one, but come with me anyway and see the lobby."

They turned and headed for the historic Lake Breeze Hotel, perched right on the beach. In only moments, they walked through the wide glass doors.

Alice hadn't been exaggerating about the dream reception. As they entered a fairyland, their heels clicked against the elegant wood floors in the six-story-tall rotunda. Shimmering tulle hung in strips from the central chandelier, and tables overflowing with candles and flowers circled the room. The bride had chosen pink with gold accents for her colors. The large circular room smelled of roses and lilies and glimmered with glass, candles, china and silverware.

Alice breathed in the effect. Too bad it was temporary. Weddings always went too fast, especially compared with the months of planning and preparation. And a wedding reception in the lobby of a working hotel had to be finite. Without a separate conference facility or hall, a reception snarled the hotel traffic. Alice's staff had one hour to move in all the carefully prepared decorations. The afternoon dessert and champagne reception would last two hours—just enough time for toasts, pictures, cutting the four-tiered cake and dancing the traditional first dances.

After that, everything would go into storage and families with beach bags and sand between their toes would again traipse through the lobby on their way to the elevators. As a thank-you to hotel guests inconvenienced by the reception, Alice made sure any fresh flowers that were left when the event ended were made into bouquets and delivered to rooms with couples celebrating anniversaries or honeymoons. She even had waiters deliver elegant plated pieces of cake to guests waiting to check in at the front desk.

Alice knew how little things could add up, and big events were just a lot of little things packed into one small section of time and space. One mistake could screw up the whole thing. It was one of the many ways weddings, she thought, differed from marriages.

"I'm definitely divorcing Mel and starting over," June said.

"Didn't you have a beautiful wedding the first time?"

June smiled. "We did. It was a Christmas wedding in the ballroom. Red roses and evergreens, a six-tiered cake and a live band. I spent a lot of time teaching Mel to dance before the reception."

Alice imagined those lessons were more fun than work, but she certainly admired June's spirit of perfection. Weddings should be perfect, right down to the dance steps.

"But he's still not as good a dancer as you, I'd bet."

"After seven seasons on Broadway, I'm tough competition."

The small orchestra that had played for the ceremony on the boardwalk came in and took their seats on the edge of the rotunda. They tuned their instruments and straightened sheet music on their stands.

In the two years Alice had coordinated special events for Starlight Point, she'd developed relationships with many local industry professionals. She was becoming a regular at the bridal shop that did expert and quick alterations. She had her own seat at the counter in Augusta's downtown bakery where she could flip through a huge portfolio of wedding cakes. Alice knew all the members of the string quintet and had four Bayside ministers on speed dial.

Alice straightened the silverware on the cake table. "Do you regret giving up the stage and coming home?"

June shook her head. "Only a tiny bit once in a while. I gained so much more than I gave up. How about you? You still live at home with your parents. Do you regret never leaving Bayside?"

"No," Alice said. She tugged a wrinkle out of a crisp white tablecloth. "Definitely, no."

There were things she regretted, but location wasn't one of them. Starlight Point was her dream job, bringing back happy memories of a time in her life when she thought she had it all figured out.

"Have you met our new public relations guy? He just started yesterday, and he's got lots of experience with updating websites, photography and networking. He's a local who just came back to the area," June said. "Maybe you know each other."

"I haven't met him yet," Alice said as she

checked the time on her phone and switched it into camera mode.

"He's supposed to come take pictures for the website, but if he doesn't hurry he'll miss the big entrance," June said. "He already missed the wedding itself."

Alice wanted to ask more about him and talk to June about how her department and his might work together, but time was tight. She walked to the glass lobby door and peered out. "They're headed this way."

She nodded to the leader of the orchestra and held up two fingers to signal he had two minutes before striking up a lively entrance piece. She and June faded to the edge of the room to wait for the bridal couple to sweep in with their family and friends. She was ready with her camera to capture the moment the bride saw the rotunda's decorations. In a word, it was perfection.

"I LIKE THE way you're jumping right into work," Jack Hamilton told Nate as he dropped him off at the Lake Breeze Hotel. "I'm glad I finally talked my sisters into hiring someone to sell us year-round."

"You make it sound cheap when you put it

like that," Nate said. "But thanks. I'm going to make sure there isn't a person in Michigan or the entire Midwest who doesn't know about the Starlight Point brand and want to be here on their next fifteen vacations."

"You better get to the wedding on time," Jack said.

"I wish I had that new camera I ordered yesterday."

"First day on the job and you're already spending money?"

"Wait until you see your new website. I promise it'll be worth it."

"Talk to my sister Evie about that," Jack said. "The queen of the accounts."

Nate got out of Jack's car, shut the door and waved to his boss. He'd admired Jack from a distance throughout high school. And he wasn't the only one. Everyone in Bayside knew the Hamiltons—the owners of the amusement park that put the whole area on the map and provided jobs for any local teenager willing to work.

When Nate had realized he'd have to come home to Bayside, he knew Starlight Point was the best and only place he could use his public relations experience.

As he dashed through the entrance of the hotel, he slid his hand into the pocket of his suit jacket to keep his smartphone from flying out. Cell phone pictures weren't the best, but his first project for the coming week was to add some life to Starlight Point's utilitarian website, so he couldn't wait for the wedding photographer's images.

The special events page needed pictures to go with the list of packages available. He glanced around the rotunda as he entered from the back of the hotel. This couple had gone all out. And he knew from studying the wedding packages available that it was just as expensive as it looked.

Whatever makes people happy. He was in the business of making things look good, and whether or not this bride and groom made it to their first anniversary was none of his concern. For today, it was perfection, and the company website would reflect that image like sunshine off a glass window.

He got ready with his cell phone, focusing on the door where everyone seemed to be waiting for the bride and groom to make a splashy entrance. June Hamilton was talking with an auburn-haired woman whose back was to him. She must be the wedding planner. Good. He needed to make friends fast if he wanted to impress the Hamiltons and make them glad they'd created a new position.

Realizing they had a better vantage point for viewing the arriving couple, Nate approached June and the other woman. He stepped behind them and said, "Hello, June. I'm glad I made it in time to get a picture. Wow, this place is—"

The red-haired woman turned around and his words disappeared. He sucked in a breath.

Alice Birmingham.

He dropped his phone and the glass screen cracked into an expensive spiderweb. While bending to pick it up, he completely missed the grand entrance of the couple and straightened in time to see Alice looking at the picture on her phone with a satisfied smile.

June leaned over to look at Alice's phone. "You got a good one," she commented. "Hi, Nate. I'm sure Alice will share it with you. She's just as invested in special events here as you are."

Alice stared at Nate and raised her eyebrow. It was only a slight consolation to notice her flushed cheeks. Was she as shocked as he was?

"Sorry," June said. "I should introduce you two. Alice Birmingham, I'd like you to meet Nate Graham. You'll be working together a lot now that Starlight Point is going big on PR and special events."

Nate extended his hand automatically and tried to play it cool in front of his new employer. He always played it cool, just as expected from a public relations expert.

While they shook hands, Nate was aware of June's interested stare. The Hamiltons were all smart, perceptive people, and it wouldn't be easy to fake a cordial relationship with Alice for long. Why, in the midst of a full-blown wedding and on his second day of a job he needed did Alice have to walk back into his life? He'd been prepared to see people from his past when he came home to Bayside. In most cases, it would be a welcome benefit to returning home so he could be the son his dad needed right now. But Alice?

"Have you two met before?" June asked.

"Yes," Alice said.

"No," Nate said at the same time.

June crossed her arms and glanced from one to the other. "Okay, so maybe."

"Bayside is a small town," Alice said.

Nate couldn't help noticing that five years had hardly changed Alice. She still had cream-colored skin and auburn hair that waved away from her face. Petite and slender, she looked as if she could be twenty, not the twenty-seven he knew her to be. Despite her delicate beauty, there was steel underneath. He'd learned that the hard way.

"When I stopped by the wedding," June said, "I was on my way to wardrobe. I'm checking on the costumes for the fall festival. I hope our head seamstress, Gloria, is still talking to me after all I've asked her to do. Maybe I can meet with both of you on Monday to talk about fall festival details." June wrinkled her nose and tilted her head. "Even if you two only maybe know each other."

Nate nodded and Alice did the same.

"Those weekends are coming up fast and we have a lot to discuss," June added. She stayed a moment more as if she had something else to say, but then she turned and left the rotunda. Nate was relieved to see her go, but his nerves still trembled, his pulse on high alert.

The orchestra played "Pachelbel's Canon in D" as the bride and groom made a sweep of the room arm in arm, greeting their guests. Everything smelled like flowers and cake, but Nate felt nothing but sick misery. Each wedding he'd attended over the past five years, as his friends had gotten married one by one, had helped toughen his defenses when it came to weddings, but he still worked to shape his expression into PR neutral.

Alice pointed toward the cracked phone in his hand. "That's not a great beginning."

"You're not exactly in a position to lecture me about beginnings."

"I'm not lecturing you," Alice said. "June wasn't kidding when she said we'd be working together. My office is right across the hall from yours."

"You're not serious."

Alice looked away and then returned her gaze to him. She bit her lip. "I'm serious about a lot of things."

"But not marriage."

"Weddings are my business now. It goes

with the special events territory at Starlight Point."

Nate laughed heartlessly, but there was so much chatter and music echoing in the room that only Alice would hear it. "Oh, the irony."

Her cheeks colored deeper, and Nate felt a tiny stab of guilt for being so harsh. Not to mention the fact that harassing a beautiful woman at a fairy-tale wedding would not look good for him or Starlight Point.

"It's not as ironic as you think," she protested. "I guess you could consider it a way to atone for what—"

"For what you did," he said bitterly.

Alice shook her head. "For what I didn't do."

Nate wished he was anywhere else. He'd often wondered what he would say if he ever saw Alice again. There was no worse time and place for this reunion than the present. He should shut his mouth and leave if he wanted to keep his emotions together and keep his job. He'd be no good to himself or his dad if he got fired on his second day working for Starlight Point.

He just had to ask one question.

"Have you ever wondered what would have

happened if you hadn't walked out on our wedding?"

Alice's shoulders dropped and she looked at the floor. "Every day for the last five years."

Without another word, Nate spun and retreated through the lobby, walking as fast as he could without running and making a spectacle of himself.

CHAPTER TWO

IN THE FIVE work days since the glorious wedding on the beach, Alice had refreshed the special events webpage ten times a day, hoping to see the pictures she had emailed to Nate Graham from her phone. She vaguely wondered if he had replaced his phone or had the screen repaired, but that was not her problem. She had plenty of problems of her own to worry about, such as making sure her events were perfect and the revenue generated was enough to ensure she kept her job.

In addition to refreshing the website, she had replayed her meeting with Nate. Of all people…Nate Graham. Why was he back in Bayside? And did she really have to plan and publicize weddings side by side with him? The fates could not have doled out a more suitable punishment if the universe was looking to mess with her perfectly ordered life.

On Friday afternoon, the previous weekend's wedding pictures finally appeared along with text describing the venue, flowers, music and food. There was an accurate description of the bride's gown, the flowered arch on the boardwalk, the size of the party, the cake and the new couple's first song. Of course it was accurate. Alice had written it herself and emailed it to Nate, who now had full control of Starlight Point's webpage and social media. Her jaw tightened when she got to the part explaining that the "staff" of Starlight Point had coordinated the event.

"I'm the staff," she muttered to herself. Along with some dedicated helpers, special events sat squarely on Alice's shoulders. Yes, there were many Starlight Point employees she called upon to set up chairs and serve food and drinks, but all the planning and worrying fell to her.

Virginia Hamilton was her right-hand woman these days. Retired, but still actively involved and interested in the amusement park she and her late husband had run for forty years, Virginia enjoyed being involved with special events. She wanted a job that would have her out and about in the parks and would be different every day.

While Virginia and Alice were staying busy bringing in people and revenue with their special events, they'd also been planning for the fall festival weekends. It was Alice's brainchild and a large part of the reason Starlight Point had hired her. She also suspected it was a large part of the reason they had decided to hire a full-time PR person.

"Great," she said as she dug through her filing cabinet. "I probably got him that job and now I have to work with him."

"Sandwiches," the office assistant, Haley, announced. "There was a line at the employee cafeteria. Sorry about the wait."

Haley was a fresh-faced eighteen-year-old working her last summer job before going off to college. She showed up early every day—even though Alice had told her it wasn't necessary—and was always happy to help. Her enthusiasm reminded Alice of being just out of high school when it seemed everything was possible.

"Thanks," Alice said. "I didn't mind the wait, but now that I think about food, I'm pretty hungry."

Haley pulled one foil-wrapped sandwich

out of the bag and put it on Alice's desk. "Eat it before it gets cold."

"In a minute. I just have to find some stuff I stashed in this filing cabinet—plans for the fall festival weekends. Those start next weekend, and I'm pretty sure we're going to need twenty-five-hour days to get everything ready."

"You'll be ready. I've seen you pull off some amazing things this summer."

"Thanks." *I can use all the encouragement I can get.*

Haley lingered in the doorway, combing her fingers through her bangs and frowning. "I'm thinking of getting blond highlights because I'm tired of my one-color hair. What do you think?"

Alice closed the filing drawer. "No way. If you just get highlights on top of your dark hair, you'll look like a baby skunk."

"Oh," the younger girl said, her smile fading.

"A very cute baby skunk," Alice said quickly. "But if you want a change, I think you should go with layers."

"Maybe you're right," Haley said.

"Or a Starlight Point tattoo," Alice said, grinning. "Someplace really obvious."

Haley shook her head. "Very funny."

"You asked. I think, in your heart, you probably thought it was a bad idea before you even heard my opinion."

"At least I know that if I do something drastic and it looks awful, I'm sure you would tell me the truth."

"I would. Unless it's a tattoo—those are permanent. I'd tell you the truth if it was something you could fix."

Haley smiled and crossed the hall to deliver Nate's lunch. She and Nate laughed and talked for a while before Haley finally said goodbye. Of course she was trying to make a good impression on Nate—she wanted to become a public relations media consultant. And Nate was charming and pleasant when he wanted to be. Because he worked in PR, he knew how to make things look and sound good.

And, she had to admit, he still looked good, unchanged by the years except for a little more muscle and maturity in his expression. Tall with dark hair and eyes, he could easily win people over, which meant they could be working together a long, long time. There was no way to avoid the problem, and she should be honest with herself, march across the hall and…say something to Nate.

Instead, she sighed, squirted some sanitizer on her hands and sat down at her desk to eat. Maybe lunch would fuel her up to face what she had to. She rolled the sandwich over and read the name written in black marker on the package. *Nate.*

Alice groaned and closed her eyes. She could eat Nate's sandwich, which, according to the wrapper, was ham, mustard and lettuce. That would mean giving up her favorite: turkey, provolone and pickles. Or she could bravely march across the hallway and trade with him.

"I believe this is yours."

She dropped the sandwich and looked up. Nate leaned on her office door, a sandwich in his hand. He had beaten her to it, and she couldn't think of a thing to say.

Instead of speaking, Alice held up the item he'd come for. He crossed her small office, took his sandwich and laid hers in front of her without a word.

"Thank you," she said.

Nate was almost to the door, but he paused and half turned. "You're welcome. I know you hate mustard."

He slipped into the hallway, leaving her no chance to respond. It was just mustard, of course, but the fact he remembered… That was going to make it twice as hard to work with the man she'd chosen not to marry only hours before their own wedding.

"I USED TO love pumpkin pie," Henry said. "But I don't think I can ever enjoy it again after this."

Virginia laughed. "It's not so bad. If we take enough painkillers tonight, we'll live to do this all over again tomorrow."

She took a small pumpkin from a wagon and tossed it to Henry. He walked to a flower-bed, glanced at a color-coded map and placed it beside a green squash.

Nearby, the midway fountain had been transformed into an autumn display of colors and textures. All summer long, refreshing spray from the light blue splash pad tempted children to play in the water and cooled the air for people passing by. The water was turned off for the fall festival, though, and a giant inflatable pumpkin crouched over the area. Children could run through the pumpkin's grinning mouth while their parents rested on the benches circling it.

In addition to the hay bales and pumpkins artfully placed around the seating area, Virginia and Henry were laying out various sizes and colors of pumpkins and squash in the flowerbed. When completed, the vegetables would create a fall landscape scene, but it took attention to detail. It reminded Virginia of the paint-by-number projects she'd done with her children during long, snowy Michigan winters.

"I better look at the diagram again," Henry said. "I don't want our artwork to look like a couple of teenagers dashed it together so they could quit early."

"Nothing against the kids," Virginia said, "but old age does have its advantages."

Henry stepped close and stood over Virginia, blocking the sun and smiling down at her. Small wrinkles around his eyes were accentuated by the smile, and she noticed one white hair mixed with his blond eyebrows.

"We are not old," he said. "Especially not you."

"Fifty-seven earlier this summer," Virginia said. Henry stood so close she could smell his soap. It was clean and practical, just like the rest of him. He had a lean, straight build and walked with confidence, as if he were a man accustomed to responsibility. She'd noticed, though, that he was happy helping out however he could, and he seemed to take pride in executing the fall displays exactly as depicted on the directions. His skill was probably a result of following flight diagrams and paying attention to detail. It was also probably a relief, she thought, to fuss over gourds instead of turbulence after years of being responsible for hundreds and thousands of lives.

She'd felt a similar relief when she handed over Starlight Point to her children Jack, June and Evie. A grieving and shocked widow at the time, she hadn't thought she could put one more thing on her plate, and she was confident her children were stronger than she was. In the five summers since her beloved Ford had succumbed to a heart attack, she'd seen for certain the strength of her three children.

And her own strength.

"I'm just a little closer to sixty than you are," Henry said, drawing her back into their conversation. "But I feel like eighty after setting out straw bales and lifting pumpkins all day yesterday."

"Is it still better than sitting in the cockpit of a plane?"

Henry ran a hand through his hair and looked down the midway as if he were considering the question. Virginia wondered if he missed his old job now that he was retired. Without a family, did he feel lonely? She'd felt as if she'd been set adrift when Ford died, but she still had her children to give her a reason to get out of bed.

"Most days, yes. It's nice not worrying about hijackers, lightning and schedules."

"We have lightning and schedules here," Virginia said.

"So I guess I feel right at home," he replied, smiling. "Just don't bring in any hijackers for my benefit."

Virginia laid a paper copy of the decoration placement diagram on the wagon's wood floor and smoothed it with both hands. "Alice saw to every detail," she said.

Henry leaned over her shoulder to view the diagram, and Virginia felt the warmth from his body. There was a touch of autumn in the air, just enough to make his warmth welcome. It had been a long time since she'd thought about men and heat in the same sentence. Or noticed what a man smelled like. Or wondered if one found her attractive.

"Mom."

Virginia turned so quickly she almost knocked Henry off his feet. Evie, blond ponytail making her look as if she were twelve and not twenty-five, handed a bottle of cold water to her and Henry. "I could get someone else to do all this physical labor."

Virginia realized her heart was racing. Was it the new awareness of Henry, a man with whom she'd worked all summer? Or was it this new consciousness being interrupted by her daughter—and making her feel guilty?

There was no reason she should feel guilty.

"You mean someone younger?" she asked Evie, keeping her tone light and playful.

Evie laughed. "That's not what I meant."

"Yes, it was."

"Maybe a little. Can I help it that I love my mother?" Evie put an arm around Virginia's shoulders, which increased her distance from Henry. He stepped back, eyes on the ground. "And, besides," Evie continued. "I don't want you to wear yourself out. You have to save energy for Gladys."

Virginia smiled at the thought of her new labrador.

Henry removed the cap from his water bottle and took a long drink. "Who's Gladys?"

"My new dog."

"New?" Henry asked.

"I had a dog named Betty for years," Virginia said.

"Roughly one hundred years," Evie added.

"She wasn't that old," Virginia protested, and then she laughed when Evie waggled her eyebrows at Henry. "Fine, she was fourteen but she was wonderful."

Evie straightened her smirk into a neutral expression. "She had many wonderful qualities in addition to her less wonderful ones."

"Don't we all?" Henry asked. "So is your new dog—?"

"Gladys," Virginia supplied.

"Gladys. Is she a puppy?"

Virginia shook her head. "She's about four or five." She'd given serious thought to a litter of puppies curled into a ball at the humane society, but then Gladys had stolen her heart.

A chocolate lab with a few years under

her belt, her soulful eyes had looked deep into Virginia's own and forged a connection. Virginia had signed the paperwork immediately and driven to her small house on the old road adjoining Starlight Point, a warm nose on her shoulder the whole way. It was nice having another living soul in the house again after being alone so long. In the few days they'd been together, she'd taken Gladys for a morning walk through Starlight Point before it opened for the day, two romps on the beachs and one trip to the pet-friendly supply store in Bayside.

"And she was already saddled with the name Gladys," Evie said. "Mom didn't pick that one."

"You could probably change it," Henry said. "Maybe to something that rhymes with Gladys so it doesn't confuse her." Virginia and Evie swung their heads in unison to stare at Henry and he held up both hands. "Don't ask me to think of something that rhymes with that."

"Already tried it. My brother thought of a few suggestions, but we had to reject them."

"I'll use my imagination," Henry said. "I've never had a dog, couldn't have one because I was never home. Wouldn't have been fair."

Virginia noticed her daughter's look of confusion and it occurred to her that she knew a substantial lot about Henry, but Evie did not. Virginia and Henry had worked together most of the summer, grilling hot dogs on the boardwalk, handing out prizes at employee game nights and manning a table at a season pass holder appreciation night. He'd shared stories of his early years flying for the air force and then his twenty-five-year career as a commercial airline pilot. While Virginia had devoted her life to Starlight Point, Henry had been all over the world.

"Why weren't you ever home?" Evie asked.

Virginia could have answered the question for him, but she listened instead while he gave Evie an account of his years in the air, his retirement and his move home to Bayside where he kept busy working at Starlight Point.

"And what do you do when you're not judging beautiful baby contests and keeping my mother out of trouble?" Evie asked.

"Nothing," Henry joked. "That's a full-time job. But I do have a 1960 Chevy pickup

I'm restoring. It's how I avoid fixing the porch door at my house. I hate doing home improvements."

"Which is why I live in a condo," Evie said. "I see now why you've never had a dog, and you probably never found time to have a dozen children either."

"No children," Henry said. "My brother and sister have kids and grandkids now, so I've enjoyed being an uncle. I show up with presents on special occasions, and I've been lucky enough to give free plane tickets to my nieces and nephews for their honeymoons. I can't complain."

Virginia thought of her honeymoon with Ford more than thirty years earlier. He'd sunk all his money into buying Starlight Point from a previous owner who'd fallen on difficult times, so their honeymoon did not involve a flight to a tropical paradise. They'd honeymooned right in the Lake Breeze Hotel. It had been substantially renovated just recently, but she still thought of her late husband when she walked through the doors into the lobby. He'd loved that hotel, just as he'd loved Starlight Point.

She hoped he'd be happy if he could somehow see it now under the expert guidance of their children. They'd built a marina, restored the theaters and hotel and added numerous special events such as the fall festival unfolding around them right now.

"Thanks for the water," Henry told Evie. "I'll get back to work."

As Henry picked up two pumpkins and walked over to one of the displays to tuck them in, Virginia took a close look at her youngest daughter. Her cheeks were pink and eyes bright. It was a mild autumn day, but not warm enough to bring color to Evie's cheeks.

"I have to tell you something," she said quietly once Henry was out of earshot.

Virginia guessed the news, but she let her daughter continue.

"I'm pregnant," Evie announced. Her feet practically danced on the pavement when she said it. Virginia pulled her close as tears sprang to her eyes.

"Oh, honey, I'm so happy!"

"We are, too. Due in March. It's still early, but I had to tell you first before everyone else finds out."

"That should be in about fifteen minutes,"

Virginia said. "And how are you feeling? Are you okay?"

"Great," Evie said. "A little yucky this morning before I got going, but I feel fine as long as I keep moving and focused."

"You'll get to take a nice break when this place closes. Although not as long as usual with the fall and winter events going on."

"I'm worried about being a mom and running this place," Evie confided. "Jack and June have done it, though, so I hope it'll be okay."

"It'll be better than okay," Virginia said. "Remember, you have help. And you'll have a beautiful son or daughter by next summer." She hugged her daughter again, unwilling to let her go for another moment.

"I should get back to the office," Evie said. "And I'll see if I can find June on my way there."

"Let's have a celebration dinner tonight," Virginia said. "My place—and don't worry, I'll order something instead of cooking."

"I'd love that. And Scott will be very happy you're not risking a kitchen fire. You know what a worrier he is."

Virginia watched Evie walk away, her

thoughts miles from the pumpkins she was supposed to be helping Henry arrange. She'd been so happy when Evie found true love with the new fire chief at Starlight Point. Scott and his sister Caroline had become part of their family, and Virginia was overjoyed to have more Christmas presents to buy every year.

Henry's shoe scraped on concrete behind her, interrupting her thoughts about buying nursery gifts for Evie and Scott. She hoped to know by December whether to put pink or blue presents under the tree.

"Everything okay?" Henry asked.

Virginia turned to him and nodded, unashamed of the tears in her eyes. "Family announcement," she said.

"None of my business," Henry said, "but I hope it's good news."

Virginia almost felt hurt that Henry thought it was none of his business. They'd become friends, she thought, with every event they'd helped put together. She wouldn't hesitate to share her good news with him—but did he consider her a friend or an employer?

A friend, she hoped. It would be public knowledge by noon the next day, and she felt no qualms sharing the excitement. She nodded. "The best kind. I'm going to have another grandchild in the spring."

Henry gave her a quick, friendly hug. "Congratulations!"

"Thanks."

Virginia felt strangely lonely when Henry released her and went back to selecting pumpkins from the pile on the wagon. He may not know what it felt like to have children and grandchildren of his own, but it had still been nice to have someone to share the joy with. She wished Ford were still here. After all, this was his grandchild, too. Pain squeezed her heart when she thought about Ford and how he would never see his grandchildren, but she swallowed the thought. Looking down the sunny midway at the roller coasters and familiar sights of Starlight Point, she knew this, too, was Ford's legacy.

And she was lucky. He'd left her so much in their three children and their shared decades of happiness. She took a deep breath. Today was a day for celebration.

"Try this one," Virginia said cheerfully, tossing a small orange pie pumpkin to Henry.

He caught it before it went sailing over his shoulder, a wide smile lighting his face.

CHAPTER THREE

NATE PASTED A smile on his face and shook hands with the photographer and writer. The *Bayside Times* wanted a story on the fall festival weekends because anything involving Starlight Point was big local news. Even bigger was the fact that the Point had never stayed open past Labor Day weekend.

"I hope you have your walking shoes on," Nate said. "In my three weeks on the job here, I've probably logged three hundred miles."

He had already replaced his expensive leather shoes from his previous job with a less flashy but much more comfortable pair of black walking shoes. He'd hated giving in and chipping away at his professional veneer, but Starlight Point had long concrete midways and long beautiful beaches. The shoes were a small concession for survival.

Many nights after running his father to chemotherapy or picking up dinner for both of them, Nate's feet still ached despite the comfortable shoes.

He'd arranged to meet the reporters at the front gate the day before the bonus weekends opened. Fall decorations were in place, but the haunted houses slated for the back of the park wouldn't open until the first of October. Despite his lack of involvement with the planning—Alice was behind all that—he already felt ownership in everything at the Point. His contribution to the company's success was the top one inch, the glossy surface that could make or break a good impression.

"Any place you'd like to start?" Nate asked.

"We want to run this in tomorrow's paper, so let's see as much as we can before lunch so we can get back to the office and write it up," the reporter, Bob, said.

Nate stood by while the photographer, Jason, took pictures of the front gates, where scarecrows, pumpkins and bales of straw were arranged. Even the tall letters spelling out the name of the park were festive. A scarecrow replaced the letter *L* in Starlight and a ghost peeked out from the letter *O* in Point. Orange and purple lights chased across the welcome marquee instead of the usual red and blue ones.

The pictures were guaranteed to convey the right message. Even the sunshine cooperated as if it were on Nate's PR payroll. There were no people with unpredictable expressions to throw a wild card into this story, just artful but inanimate objects that were easily controlled.

"Looks like you're ready," Bob commented. "Any projections on attendance figures? I bet the owners are banking on this paying off."

Nate smiled. "Starlight Point considers itself an important part of the community and is excited to extend the season and welcome guests. Season pass holders will continue to get in free, and we hope they bring their friends and families for fall fun."

The reporter cocked his head and grinned. "Sounds like the official company line instead of a hard answer."

"It is. You know we don't release numbers," Nate continued. "Starlight Point is about the experience people have, and that's tough to quantify." He had researched the last five years of press releases and articles in local papers and magazines devoted to amusement parks and tourism in the area, so he knew the company position and agreed with it. "But if you come back this weekend, you may see for yourself how many people are here."

"Plan to," Jason said. "My kids love this place."

The lone security guard at the front entrance held open one of the gates between the turnstiles while the group went through. In addition to a colorful spread of pumpkins and fall decorations, the midway carousel greeted them with skeletons affixed to every third horse in the outside row.

"Nice," Jason said, setting up a shot of a whimsical skeleton wearing a Starlight Point ball cap with its bony fingers wrapped around the brass pole. "Love the ghost riders." *Halloween lite*, Nate thought. That was a strategy he could respect.

"Plenty more decorations and thrills this way," Nate said. He led them up onto the cable car platform, where guests would board the cars and ride to the other end of the midway. "The ride's not operating today," Nate continued, "but from here, you can see all the decorations down the midway. We've gone all out making this place an autumn extravaganza."

The group stood at the edge of the platform where they could see that the flower gardens down the midway had been replaced with displays meant to be enjoyed from the air. The largest circular garden just a short distance away used orange and white pumpkins to create a picture of a grinning skull. From the ground, it would look like piles of pumpkins. *The trick is in the perspective.*

"I'll tell you a secret," Nate said, smiling. "Trade secret we'd rather you didn't print." He paused as if he was about to reveal that the genuine elephant ears came frozen or the live show performers were only lip syncing. He had their attention and relished it for a moment. Reporters, he thought, were a necessary evil. "It's the squirrels. They're cute, but they seem to believe we've set out a banquet of autumn produce for them. We've already had to replace dozens of pumpkins when squirrels chewed holes in the top. We may have to hire a teenager to be full-time squirrel patrol."

"Lousy resume builder," the photographer

commented. "I'd hate to see that on a job application."

As they stood on the platform with a full view of the midway, Nate saw Alice leave the corporate office with two men. He knew it was her, even from a distance, because her auburn hair caught the autumn sunshine. She also wore a pink dress he'd seen her wear at least once before. A memory of her wearing a pink prom dress while her parents snapped dozens of pictures of them raced, unwelcome, through his mind. He was glad he'd never seen her in her wedding dress because an image like that would be harder to suppress.

Where was she going with those two men? Nate tried to remember what was on the special events and weddings calendar. He controlled the company website, blog and calendars. Making himself indispensable and forging a permanent career—no matter what happened with his father—had been his goal when he'd first returned home. And then he'd found Alice right in the middle of his nice neat plan.

Aside from making sure news of Starlight Point got reported on social media, news outlets and the corporate website, he tried not to overlap or get involved with Alice. It was better that way, for both of them. Not that he owed her any favors. His goal was to protect himself, not spare her. He knew she was capable of taking care of herself.

"Ready to see the food stands and their fall theming?" Nate asked, anxious to shift his thoughts back to his job.

"Sure." The photographer put the lens cap on his camera and both men followed Nate down the steps of the cable car platform. They spent the next half hour checking out the menu boards for the food vendors, which included pumpkin pie and ghost-shaped cookies at Augusta's Midway Bakery, and spiced apple cider at Hank's Hot Dogs. At Tosha's Ice Cream stand, the reporter looked skeptically at the fall offerings. "Cinnamon squash ice cream?" he asked.

"I haven't tried it yet," Nate confessed. "I may stick with the pumpkin pie and apple fritters at the bakery."

He led the reporter and photographer down the midway, past the Sea Devil roller coaster and the new double coaster that had opened at the beginning of the season. The Shooting Star and Super Star combined a kiddie coaster track winding through and alongside a wild coaster for brave riders meeting the taller height requirement.

Nate had been out of the area when it opened, but he'd seen the media reports. Although it was a risk for the park to invest so much money in an unusual coaster, it had paid off in rider numbers and increased daily ticket sales—even though those numbers stayed in the corporate office building.

Starlight Point was on a roll, and remaining open throughout the fall weekends and then again for Christmas weekends was one sign of their fiscal bravery. Alice had talked them into the bold plan, information Jack had shared with Nate in his first week on the job.

Funny how a woman who wouldn't go through with her own life-altering event managed to talk the three Hamilton siblings into taking a massive risk with their family legacy. It wasn't his decision what the Hamiltons chose to do, but the fall and winter weekends were the reason he had something to tell the media. Public relations, he thought, were a whole lot less complicated than private ones.

Near the Wonderful West Railroad Station, Nate had set up a family and friends picture zone. It was an idea he'd borrowed from his last job, at a large amusement park a thousand miles away. Even though he'd never thought he'd come home and work locally, he wasn't coming home empty-handed.

Seeing the photo spot set up with hay bales for families to sit on surrounded by bright orange pumpkins reminded him of a family photo taken when he was eight, his sister was eleven and his mother was alive. His family had sat on hay bales at a local apple farm and had their picture taken. Nate had a copy of that picture on his desk in his office. *If only I could go back in time.*

As Nate and his group crossed the train tracks and entered the Western Trail, the decorations shifted from cheerful pumpkins and mazes made of straw bales to spiderwebs and glaring scarecrows. The haunted houses and spooky trails were planned for the back of the park so parents of young children would have no trouble avoiding the scary parts if they chose. Teenagers and adults who wanted to appear brave in front of their friends could bypass children's games and experience the fall celebration with a much higher thrill rating.

Bats swung from trees, spiderwebs covered the buildings on the Western Trail, and an arch with a creepy skull with red glowing eyes welcomed them to the Dark Trail of the Undead. Eerie music played even though the park wasn't open.

"Not sure I like this," Bob said.

"I know what you mean. It's going to be blood-chilling and definitely not for everyone," Nate said. He shuddered.

"Are you kidding?" the photographer asked. "This is the best part. I'm getting a babysitter and coming back here with my wife as soon as the haunted houses open for real."

"You won't be disappointed." Nate led them down the trail, pausing when the photographer lagged behind to take pictures. "You'll see the carousel in the Wonderful West is in the process of being transformed, and I'll give you a sneak preview outside the shooting gallery, which will be a haunted house."

"Slow down so I can get a candid picture of you showing us around. It would be great if you'd look scared," Jason said.

Nate controlled his expression and managed a smile. *No way.*

"It's not about me. It's about our guests," he said. He turned and resolved to keep his face out of the photographer's lens. He'd rather be the one controlling the news.

As they passed over a small bridge in the Wonderful West and approached the old-fashioned western-themed carousel, Nate saw a flash of pink among the carousel horses. He herded his group that way, not sure if it was the best or worst plan. Maybe Alice would take Mr. Camera-Happy off his hands. No matter his feelings about her, she was clearly a far more attractive subject than he was.

She stood between two carousel horses, chatting easily with a couple of men who must be from the haunted house production company. Not exactly corporate types, the men wore faded jeans and company T-shirts. One had a demented clown tattoo on his arm and the other had a week's worth of beard.

Starlight Point was hiring them for their talent, not their personal image.

Alice looked up and saw Nate, and her smile faltered for a moment. Then it flashed back. Nate considered making an excuse and racing in the other direction, but he had to be around her sometime. Might as well take this opportunity to practice appearing to have a cordial relationship.

Appearances, as any PR specialist knew, were a powerful moderator of behavior. And he needed all the help he could get.

"NATE," ALICE SAID, stepping down from the platform of the carousel. "I'm glad your group ran into mine this morning."

She juggled her bag and a pile of papers and extended a hand to the reporter and photographer from the *Bayside Times*. "Alice Birmingham, special events coordinator for Starlight Point," she said. "I believe we've met before, but it's always nice to welcome the local press." Why hadn't Nate told her he was bringing in reporters? She would have prepared statements for them with details about the special fall events she'd spent the early half of the year planning.

She smiled toward Nate with raised eyebrows as if to say, *You can try shutting me out, but we work for the same team.*

"We're getting a tour of the decorations and games for the fall festival," Bob said.

"Well then, you haven't seen the half of it. These gentlemen are with the haunted house production company." She introduced everyone and waited for the handshaking to finish. "We decided to hire professionals to set up our haunted houses because this is the first time Starlight Point has attempted something like this. We want to get it right and scare the stuffing out of our guests."

"That's where we come in," the bearded man said. "People who walk in to our haunted houses tend to run out. Strangely, they get right back in line to do it again." He shrugged. "Fearless people are our bread and butter."

"So what kind of magic are you working here?" Bob asked.

The man from the haunted house company glanced at Alice. "How much do you want me to say?"

She smiled. "The truth, but not the whole truth. Just enough for an article that will make people wish these haunted houses were opening now instead of in a month."

While the fright designer talked with the reporters and gave them an overview of the haunted carousel and the transformation of the arcade building, Alice moved closer to Nate and whispered, "How is your tour going?"

"Fine," he said, not even looking at her.

So much for being on the same team.

"My meeting is also going well. Thanks for asking," she said quietly. She waited for his reaction, but he didn't give her a thing. This was going to be hard.

"These guys have terrifying minds," she continued, undaunted by Nate's stone face. "Exactly what we need for this project."

"I'm sure you're right."

"Don't you like haunted houses?" She remembered going through one with him while they were still in high school. They'd held each other close and laughed all the way through it. Had he liked it at the time or had he pretended to for her sake?

Nate shook his head just enough for Alice to notice. "I think real life is frightening enough most of the time."

His tone implied that *she* was one of those frightening things. Her cheeks heated and the sensation radiated down her neck. With her auburn hair and pink dress, she was afraid she'd look like a boiled blushing lobster in a moment. She didn't need his approval or even his friendship. After what happened five years ago, any kind of a relationship with Nate would require a miracle.

But she didn't need to be treated as if she was public enemy number one.

"Would you say the haunted house is intended for all ages, like a family attraction?" the reporter asked.

"Everything at Starlight Point is family oriented," Nate said.

"But there's no way I'd take my little niece into one of these haunted houses," Alice said.

"So…it's not for all ages," Bob said.

Nate cut Alice a look he might have given someone who ruined a surprise party by spilling the beans ahead of time.

"Look at this," the haunted house man said to the reporter. He swiped through several screens on his phone, turned it sideways and showed it to the men from the *Bayside Times*.

"Whoa," Jason said. "That man looks like he just saw his own funeral."

The haunted house man laughed. "Seriously, look at their faces. We know how to scare them." He turned to Alice and Nate. "Want to see these pictures of a haunted house we did in Tennessee last year?"

Alice was about to agree, her curiosity excited by the reaction of the reporters. But Nate said, "No," in a cold, determined voice.

Everyone in the group looked at him, and he put on a winning smile. "I can't wait to see the final product for myself. Don't want to ruin it by looking at pictures of similar ones."

The reporter and photographer shrugged and went back to looking at the pictures on the phone.

Alice shifted the stack of papers and folders she held so she could find a press kit from the haunted house company. It was the perfect thing to hand to the local media.

Suddenly, a breeze caught the edge of her papers and sent the top ones flying. When she tried to grab for them, the rest of the pile started to slide, and Alice's shoulder bag skated down her arm. In a moment, everything would be on the ground or flying through the air.

Surprised by the sudden breeze and soaring papers, Alice was even more shocked when Nate deftly caught two papers midair and used his other hand to right her stack before it spiraled to the ground and spread out in a paperwork tsunami. Nate took the strap of her bag and put it back on her shoulder. As he helped her balance her pile of papers, his hand touched hers and he jerked it back as if he'd been burned. He flushed red and stepped back.

The other men stopped their conversation to stare.

"Paper cut," Nate said. He locked eyes with Alice for a moment and the expression she saw in his eyes looked like panic.

Come on. Am I really that much of an ogre?

"Those are wicked," the reporter said. "Paper cuts."

Nate swallowed and nodded. "The worst."

Alice took her bag off her shoulder and shoved all the papers in it. She didn't even care about wrinkling them. She'd ask Haley to print new ones if she had to.

"I think we're ready to move on to the haunted house in the shooting gallery," she said pleasantly to her two consultants. She smiled at the reporter and photographer. "I don't want to hold you up any longer. I'm sure you have a lot more ground to cover and a story to put out today."

"We have plenty of material already, but I wouldn't mind seeing what's going on inside the shooting gallery," Bob said. "People in town are pretty curious about what you're cooking up here at the Point. I think you're going to have a big success on your hands."

"I sure hope so. I was one of the people who talked the Hamiltons into staying open all fall, so I'll feel responsible if it doesn't go well. As the special events coordinator, nothing is better than a happy ending."

She heard Nate cough but didn't glance his way. Instead, Alice squared her shoulders and focused on the reporter. "I can't wait to tell you about the events we have planned for Christmas. I can't say much now, but you might have noticed there's a very large parking lot out front that would be perfect for something such as—" she put one finger on her chin and looked to the sky "—perhaps an ice skating rink or a Christmas tree lot."

The reporter laughed. "Next you'll be telling me you're bringing in live reindeer and authentic elves."

"I can't reveal company secrets," she said. "But if you know anyone who wants to get married, you can tell them there may be one weekend in December that isn't booked yet for a Christmas wedding."

Jason turned to the reporter and elbowed him. "Hear that, Bob? Maybe you and Shelly should make it official?"

"Shelly's mother hasn't learned to like me yet," Bob said. "Maybe next year. In the meantime, how about letting us inside the haunted house?"

Alice shook her head. "Sorry, we want to keep some surprises for our guests."

"We'll walk with you as far as the arcade," Nate said. He flashed a smile at the reporters. "But we'll have to behave ourselves and not crash the party. There's plenty of time for going through the haunted house when it opens."

The group of six started walking in a disorganized blob. She wanted to walk between the two men from the haunted house company so she could talk freely with them as she had been for the past hour or so. But she didn't dare tell the *Bayside Times* to put their cameras and notebooks away and head home, no matter how much she wanted to.

At the steps of the Western Arcade, she conceded to smiling for a picture with the haunted house producers. Now would they go?

"You might just see yourself in tomorrow's

paper," the photographer said congenially. "But it sure would be a better picture if you were inside and we got a glimpse of something scary."

Alice laughed, but then she noticed Nate's expression as he stood behind the reporters. His usual pleasant, polite PR man veneer had been wiped off as if someone used an eraser on a chalkboard. He swallowed hard and glared at her.

Was he possessive about the news that came out of Starlight Point, or did a picture giving her credit for the fall events burn his biscuits that badly?

CHAPTER FOUR

THE NEXT DAY'S newspaper was on Alice's doorstep by seven in the morning. The doorstep actually belonged to her parents, whose house she still lived in. Alice had been a year-round employee at Starlight Point for two years after working her way up to the coveted position by many summers of seasonal employment. Waiting tables in the off-season hadn't been profitable, but she'd gotten by and taken pride in paying back her own student loans.

She might even have afforded her own place, but she'd been meticulously putting aside a portion of her paycheck every month to repay her parents for the wedding she'd called off the night before it happened. They had already paid for the flowers, the church, the reception facility, the band, the dress and the cake. How had she let them and herself get so carried away and run up such a giant bill? Maybe she wouldn't be regretting the thousands of dollars spent if she'd gone through with the wedding.

In a few more months, she could surprise her parents by repaying the entire cost of disappointing them in one fell swoop. Then, at twenty-seven, she could finally get her own place, wonderfully free of the past.

She grabbed the paper from the same patch of front porch it had been thrown on by a succession of paper carriers all her life. She had about five minutes to glance through it before her father would ask for the paper with his coffee. And she knew better than to wrinkle it or mix up the sections. Her older sister had never cared to read the paper, but her younger sister had a habit of turning the sections inside out as she read them, a quirk that had spurred at least one family squabble.

She scanned the front page and was not surprised to see a big article about the fall festival weekends, which opened in a few hours. There were three pictures. One photograph of the front gate with its clever decorations, most of which had been her idea. One picture of the giant inflatable pumpkin where the midway fountain usually spewed water all summer. The massive balloon children could run through was also her idea. The third image was of a building on the Western Trail adorned with spiderwebs and bats. No pictures of Alice or anyone else.

"Is the paper here?" her father called from the kitchen.

I've got to get my own subscription, she thought. She resolved to read the article online as soon as she got to her office.

An hour later, Alice was glued to her laptop screen, skimming the article and hoping— vain though it was—to see a glimpse of her name, just so she could revel in the feeling of doing something right.

"Come on," she said. She scrolled past an obnoxious flashing ad and kept reading to the end of the piece. Her shoulders fell. There was no mention of her in the article. Despite her hard work, imagination and planning. Despite the fact she had personally helped inflate that stupid pumpkin balloon.

"You don't look happy," Haley said. She put a cup of coffee on Alice's desk. "It's from Augusta's bakery. I got you the good stuff because it's opening day for the fall festivals."

"Thank you," Alice said. She still continued to skim the article, hoping she'd just missed it.

"Is something not going well?"

Alice shook her head. "Everything's going fine with the opening, I think. It's something else."

Haley stepped around Alice's desk and looked at her computer screen. "I saw that article in the paper while I waited for the coffee to brew at Augusta's. I tried reading it to distract myself from getting a doughnut. My strategy failed, but the article seems like great publicity."

"For Starlight Point, yes."

Haley raised an eye brow and waited.

Alice sighed. "Sorry. Yes, it's good PR for the Point. I just hoped… It's silly—"

"They didn't even mention your name after all the work you did."

"You noticed that, too."

"I did. I guess it's good that the attitude around here is all for one and one for all, isn't it?" Haley sat on the edge of Alice's desk. "Why do you think your name wasn't mentioned? It's obvious the Hamiltons really like and value your work."

"They didn't interview me or the Hamiltons. Only one person contributed to that article."

"Nate," Haley said. She cocked her head as if trying to figure something out.

Alice nodded. "I'm taking this way too personally," she said.

"Does Nate have something against you?"

Alice hesitated. "The short answer to that question is yes. The long answer is something I'd rather not talk about."

Haley raised both eyebrows. "Must be a good story there."

"More like a cautionary tale," Alice replied.

EIGHT HOURS LATER, Nate checked his watch, hoping the weekend event would start on time. During the fall festival weekends, the park would be open Friday evenings and all day Saturday and Sunday. As the sun slanted across the sprawling parking lot at five o'clock on Friday, a sizable crowd gathered outside the front gate. Most of them wore jeans and sweatshirts as the September evenings already had the chill of fall.

Nate stood beside Virginia and Henry—keeping them between him and Alice. In the few weeks he'd worked at Starlight Point, Nate had discovered Henry was a good friend. Most of Nate's friends had moved away from the area, and even though he'd come home to be an anchor for his dad, Nate felt he was drifting.

Jack, June and Evie Hamilton shared a microphone at the front gate and each of them said a few words about the extended season. Jack pointed to Alice who was standing only a few feet away and publicly thanked her for being the mastermind behind the fall weekends. She blushed and gave a little wave to the crowd. Her pink jacket made her stand out in the small crowd of year-round employees who were being recognized—mostly department heads and art and design staff.

A group of performers plucked from the singers and musicians in live shows—those who hadn't yet gone back to college—performed the national anthem, and then the turnstiles opened.

"We did it," June said as she came over to Alice and Virginia. Guests poured through the front gates behind her. "I know your hard work is going to pay off."

Nate watched June hug Alice and then her

mother. He felt a twinge of guilt that he'd asked the reporter to leave Alice's name out of the article and not include the picture of her with the haunted house designers. He'd made up a story about Starlight Point wanting to recognize the team effort, not an individual's. But that wasn't his real reason.

The last thing his father needed as he battled cancer was to imagine his son was revisiting a dark period in his past. Even if that past was long over.

"Quite an event," Henry said. "Exciting."

"The first of many if it all goes well."

Henry leaned on a post and regarded Nate. "Think you'll be around for all those?"

"I'll be around as long as I need to be." The first of many cancer treatments had begun only days before, and Nate already saw the long road stretching out before him. Although his sister wanted to help, she had a young family and a job an hour away from Bayside. Nate was the obvious and willing choice for helping his dad get through the second worst experience of his life.

"You're a good son, coming home to help your father through a rough patch."

"He's the only parent I have," Nate said,

and then he caught himself. What made him reveal something so personal to a man he hardly knew? Even in his own family, Nate never talked about his mother's accident anymore. He cleared his throat. "How did you know I was...uh...helping my dad?"

"Jack told me. He didn't say much more than that."

"It's not just a rough patch," Nate said. "It's a road ten miles long." Nate hesitated a moment, afraid to share too much with Henry. "But we'll get down it okay."

The crowd around them thinned, and Alice and Virginia walked off. His conversation with Henry wasn't likely to be overheard, but it still paid to be cautious.

"I'm sorry about that," Henry said, putting a hand on Nate's shoulder. "I'm coming home again, too, after a life on the road and in the skies. Inherited my parents' place in Bayside. Most days I love it, but some days remind me it's tough to come home again."

Nate nodded, but he didn't reply. He'd already said too much.

Henry patted Nate's shoulder and then dropped his hand. "The longer I live, though, the more I know everything gets easier with time. Sometimes you just have to wait for it."

Virginia waved to Henry from across the midway as crowds of people walked between them. Henry raised a hand and waved back.

"All the Hamiltons have been terrific to work with," Nate said, glad to turn the conversation away from himself. "I hope these fall weekends pay off."

"Alice has been working on it nonstop, except for the weddings part. I think June had to talk her into adding the weddings when the Hamiltons realized what a great market it was. Easy money, I guess, since people spend ferocious amounts of money on getting married."

"Good business," Nate agreed. "And free PR. If the wedding guests leave with a great impression of Starlight Point, it's a win all around."

Across the midway, Virginia and Alice parted ways, and the older lady came over to Nate and Henry. "It's going to be a great weekend, weather-wise," she said, smiling broadly.

"Are you working tomorrow morning?" Henry asked.

She shook her head. "Not until later in the day. I'm having breakfast with the kids downtown at Augusta's bakery."

"I love that place," Henry said.

Nate noticed Henry's eager tone. Was he hoping for an invitation? Nate knew Henry and Virginia were friends, and he'd noticed them working together on numerous special events.

Virginia's expression sobered. "We love it, too, and Augusta finds us a spot in her side room where we won't be disturbed. We have family business to discuss."

"Well," Henry said. "Doughnuts will make even business a lot more pleasant."

"I didn't say it wasn't pleasant. It's been five years since my husband died, and we had to put a few things in place at the time that have run their course now," Virginia said. "In a good way."

Nate watched the crowds passing and wished he wasn't in the middle of an awkward conversation. Although Virginia wasn't his boss and had, in fact, handed over ownership to her three children equally, Nate felt uncomfortable and a little sorry for Henry because he'd been subtly shot down.

"I hope you have a nice breakfast," Henry said congenially, "and maybe I'll see you later in the day."

Virginia smiled and gave them both a little wave as she walked away.

"Piloting a jet is easier than navigating personal relationships," Henry said.

"You're telling me," Nate agreed. "That's why I save myself a lot of trouble by avoiding them."

CHAPTER FIVE

THE WEDDING FESTIVITIES were only moments from starting.

Alice had already heard the bride and groom's story, and it was one of her favorites so far. Two lovers who had met one summer working at the Point wanted to get married on the old-fashioned train that chugged around the perimeter of Starlight Point, giving low-thrill rides and scenic views to thousands of people a day. The bride had spent a summer loading and unloading passengers, and the groom had been a conductor giving a colorful spiel over the train's public address system.

Whereas most of the weddings she planned seemed overblown and overly expensive, she liked the sentimentality of this one. When they'd met in her office months earlier to talk about the wedding, Alice had cautioned them that the only way a wedding on the train would work was to have it early Friday afternoon before the gates opened at five o'clock for the evening fall festival. With special permission from the Hamiltons, Alice had lined up employees to shovel coal and operate the train. She'd had the benches removed from one of the open-air train cars and replaced with several rows of chairs for immediate family and the wedding party to witness the ceremony.

Alice and Nate planned to be one car back overseeing the unusual event and taking photographs for the company website. The orchestra was already set up in the second car and the two remaining cars awaited guests. The entire train would make two low-speed circuits of the park while the ceremony occurred, and then guests would disembark at the station in the Wonderful West where a tent was set up for a reception.

"I think this has potential for disaster," Nate said. "Who ever heard of getting married on a moving train?"

"It's not the weirdest wedding I've been approached about," Alice returned. "At least it makes more sense than getting married on a roller coaster."

"Gotta be a metaphor in that," Nate commented.

Alice rolled her eyes. "It's our job to give people what they want. As a public relations man, I'd think you'd be all about that."

Nate studied Alice with a long stare.

"Sometimes people don't know what they want," he said. "They just act like they do until it's too late."

A familiar stab of embarrassment, regret and guilt carved a path across Alice's chest. "It's never too late to be honest about what you want."

Nate's expression didn't waver, but his ears turned pink.

"Here they come," Alice said as a throng of people in formal clothes approached. They had entered the park through the marina gate where the parking lot had been reserved, and the bride and groom led the pack. "Get ready with your camera."

Nate snapped pictures of the group's arrival. The groom wore a dark suit and the bride's white gown billowed in the autumn sunshine. Wedding guests fanned out behind them as the group approached. Although it was quite an entrance, Alice was sorry to miss the wonder-eyes moment when the bride and groom first saw each other. The traditional walk down the aisle wasn't there, but holding hands and walking together toward their ceremony almost seemed better.

Maybe this marriage was about more than just the splashy ceremony. She wished all of them were.

"If I ever get married," Haley said, "I think it will be on the cable cars. I'll toss rose petals out and shower people below on the midway."

"Very romantic," Alice said. "And expensive."

Haley frowned.

"But fragrant and memorable," Alice added. "Unique."

Haley smiled. "I'd be afraid to hire you to plan my wedding. If I looked fat in my dress or my veil was a big mistake, you'd probably tell me."

Alice laughed. "Maybe not. But I would tell you if I thought you were marrying a big jerk."

Nate cleared his throat behind Alice and she felt a wave of nausea. Of course she hadn't meant to say *he* was a big jerk. She'd called off their wedding for some good reasons, but none of them involved him being a Neanderthal or a horse's hind end.

As the wedding party and other guests arrived, Alice directed them to their train cars. The bride and groom had requested an authentic old-time experience for the wedding, so each guest had a train ticket with their car and seat number in fancy script. Alice and Haley had created over one hundred of the unique tickets. The train cars were decorated with purple bunting and flowers. Bridesmaids wore strapless short purple dresses, and the groomsmen wore suits. Not terribly formal, but appropriate for an afternoon outdoor wedding.

As the guests boarded the cars, Alice noticed that most of them were in their midtwenties like the bride and groom. They were about her age, and many were wearing wedding bands. *Good for them.*

It took the efforts of Nate, Alice and Haley to get the guests in the correct rows. It should have been easy—each row of bench seats in the train cars was numbered with an ornate purple sign—but several of the guests wanted to vie for a better seat closer to the car where the ceremony would be held.

"After you," Nate said as he waited for Alice to board their car. He didn't take her arm or offer to hold her bag of supplies as she climbed up the two steps, but he stood silently with a completely neutral expression.

Did they teach that bland *everything's fine* expression in public relations classes? Nate had it down to a science.

Maybe he was right and everything *was* fine. The conductor blew the whistle, and the train lurched into motion. Alice and Nate stood by the rails of the second car, right behind the orchestra. The usual quintet was supplemented by several more instruments to guarantee enough volume to compete with train noise and wind. They played a traditional wedding march, and Alice held on to a post supporting the train car's roof to watch the ceremony unfold.

It's going well. The bride and groom met under a garland of flowers suspended from the ceiling and kept their balance thanks to a flower-covered railing. Their small bridal party sat in the front row of white chairs and parents and immediate family were right behind.

Nate smiled at Alice. "It's different, that's for sure."

"Every wedding is unique," she whispered. She listened to the vows over the train's public address system. Despite a few railroad puns, the vows were in substance, much like the ones Alice had heard dozens of times. The bride's long brown hair was arranged in a complicated twist with a short veil attached to the back. Purple ribbons wove through her hair and edged the hem of her gown. The groom teetered a little as he turned to take the ring from his best man's outstretched hand. His boutonniere slipped sideways with the quick movement, but otherwise the wedding was flawless.

As the train passed through the Wonderful West station for the first time, the bride and groom kissed. Alice breathed a sigh of relief. The ceremony was officially over. Now all they had to do was enjoy a full circuit of Starlight Point while the orchestra played, and then they'd all disembark for the reception.

"They went through with it," Nate whispered to Alice when the minister made the final proclamation.

Alice cut him a glance. "I'm happy for them."

Nate gripped the railing. "We used to ride this train when we were—"

"Younger," Alice said, before he could use a more powerful word such as *lovers* or *engaged*. Nate's expression held a trace of sadness, even vulnerability in the set of his lips and the line between his eyebrows.

The photographer in the first car aimed his camera in Alice and Nate's direction, and Nate's expression immediately flashed to PR neutral.

Everything's fine.

It was now. She had a job she loved, a future and a life of her own in Bayside. There was no point in speculating about how it might all have been different.

The train passed Virginia and Henry, who stood waiting by the large white reception tent, and Alice waved. Their presence assured Alice that every detail had been followed to the letter. She'd be glad when everyone was off the train and under the tent. She already had a bus lined up to pick up all the guests at four o'clock and return them to their cars in the marina lot. That would give her crew an hour to clean up from the reception and remove everything but the tent for the evening festival.

Thank goodness the haunted houses weren't opening for another two weeks. There wouldn't be much foot traffic in the Wonderful West on a Friday evening, and it gave her crew just a touch of breathing room in case things did not go exactly according to plan.

Alice leaned on the railing as far away from Nate as she could manage and watched the familiar scenery go past. She'd been on the train ride dozens of times and knew a fake shoot-out with mechanically animated skeletons was just around the next bend. Even though she knew it was coming, she was still startled every time the pretend guns fired.

Just as the western town came into view, Alice heard shouting from the back of the train. Two men were out of their seats in the last car having an ugly verbal exchange. Nate saw it, too, and he and Alice went to the back of their car, watching in horror as two wedding guests drew back their fists to take a swing at each other.

"Gotta be kidding me," Nate muttered. He swung a long leg over the back rail of their train car and jumped onto the car behind them. He was going to make his way back there on a moving train? Alice wanted to follow, but her close-fitting dress and high-heeled pumps wouldn't allow her to swing gracefully along the edge of the train car as Nate was now doing.

The two men in the back car were grappling while horrified guests scooted away. One man was trying to stop them, holding out his hands and shouting. Alice got out her cell phone and called the Starlight Point police department. "Fight on the train," she said. "Two wedding guests. We're just passing behind the Lake Breeze Hotel right now."

Nate had jumped to the rear car by that time and Alice watched him work his way down the side of it. He got to the fighting men just as one of them took a wild swing and fell off the train. Alice made a split-second decision, summoned her courage and jumped off the moving train. Someone had to see if the man was injured. She thought she might land on her feet because she had some athletic experience. Years of figure skating had given her poise and balance and decent jumping ability.

However, it was her first time jumping from a moving train and she completely failed to estimate the difficulty level. She tumbled and flailed, gravel flew, and she came to rest in a thick scratchy brush.

What have I done? She opened her eyes and saw the train disappearing around the next curve. A man dropped to his knees beside her and slid his arms under her. He brushed her hair back from her face. "Are you all right?"

In her scrambled state, Alice was afraid for a second it was the fighting man and he was going to take a swing at her. She risked a look at this face.

Nate's dark eyes stared into hers and his hand was gentle on her cheek. *He must have jumped off the train right after I did.*

"If I close my eyes, can I pretend nothing happened?" Alice asked.

She heard Nate's low laughter. "That's my job, finding a way to gloss this over."

He helped her sit up and continued to kneel next to her. "Your dress…" he said, gesturing to a long tear starting from the hem and going halfway up her thigh.

Alice grabbed the edges of the fabric and

held them together. Her rose-colored shift was destroyed. She just hoped the rest of it was still decent. Nate took a handkerchief from his suit pocket and dabbed at scratches on Alice's neck and shoulder. "Superficial, but I bet they sting like crazy," he said. He handed her the cloth. "Do you think anything is broken?"

"The heel off one of my shoes," she said as she glanced down and realized her favorite pumps were ruined, "and my personal pride will never be the same."

"First time jumping off a train?" he asked.

She nodded and found a smile, despite the unexpected twist of the themed wedding.

"We're not alone," Nate said. One of the fighting men was walking toward them along the tracks. Nate stood and put himself between Alice and the stranger.

"Stop right there," Nate said. "The police will be here in just a minute, and I will personally make sure you answer for this."

Nate took off his suit jacket and handed it behind him to Alice. "Use my phone and call Henry to let him know what's coming on the train."

Alice found his phone in the pocket of his

coat, which was still warm and smelled like Nate—a damp forest smell that reminded her he loved the outdoors. A memory of a camping trip they'd gone on flashed over her. As they'd sat by a fire watching the flames, he'd shared some of his grief over his mother's passing and she'd felt as if she really knew him for the first time. But when the campfire died, he was back to pretending he was fine.

Alice pushed aside the memory and called Henry. She gave him a quick warning and told him to make sure the Starlight Point police officers knew the description of the person they were looking for.

Alice struggled to her feet and swayed a little. She put a hand to her forehead, reminding herself to take a deep breath and assess the actual damage. Nate slid an arm around her and held her against his chest while he kept an eye on the other man. He didn't look at her, just held her as if she were a pillow or a bag of groceries.

Two Starlight Point police officers came through the trees and bushes separating the train tracks from the rear parking lot of the Lake Breeze Hotel.

"There's your man," Nate said. The officers walked over to the assailant. The fight had apparently gone out of him with his wild swing and fall from the train. His shoulders slumped and he kept his hands up in surrender. One of the officers cuffed him anyway.

"Got two cars in the hotel lot. I'll take him to the station," an officer said. "You two can ride in the other car and we'll write up the report."

Nate bent to pick up his suitcoat from the ground. One of the sleeves was torn. He put the coat over Alice's shoulders.

"I'm not cold," she protested.

"You need to look decent in case anyone's watching."

Despite his cool tone, he kept an arm around her as they picked through the bushes and trees to the waiting police cars.

Nate held open the front passenger side door of the police car and closed it after Alice got in. She took Nate's coat and laid it across her lap to cover the lengthy exposure of leg under her ripped dress. It was bad enough Nate had seen it; she didn't want to feel exposed and vulnerable in front of anyone else, especially the cop, who was several years younger than she was.

After he got in the back seat, Nate leaned forward. "If any cell phone video of that fracas emerges on social media, I'm going to claim it was staged to make an authentic Wild West–themed wedding train even more exciting."

Alice laughed, amused and horrified at the same time.

The young police officer got in the driver's seat. "Do you two need medical attention? I could run you past first aid on the way to the police station."

"I'm fine," Nate said from the back seat, "but Alice may need someone to take a look at her."

She shook her head. "I'm fine. I'd like to get back to the wedding."

The officer raised an eyebrow. Of course she'd get cleaned up and changed first. She knew she probably didn't look anywhere close to being presentable. "Might be a while," he said. "I heard on the radio they're bringing in a man and a woman they picked off the train at the Wonderful West station. Might be a lovers' spat we have to sort out and decide who's pressing charges where."

"A crime of passion," Nate said softly from

the back seat. "Those make good stories, just not what we need at Starlight Point."

WHEN THEY GOT to the Starlight Point police station, June and Evie Hamilton were waiting for them. Nate ushered Alice in and let his eyes adjust to the dim interior of the station. The bright sun of the September afternoon had been blinding, and his head was starting to throb. He'd never jumped off a moving train before, and he was sure he'd whacked his head somewhere along the way. Maybe that explained why he felt so disoriented.

"What happened to you?" June exclaimed when she saw Alice.

"I jumped from the train when one of the fighters fell off," she explained. Alice gestured toward Nate, who was standing behind her. "He jumped off, too."

"I hope you're both okay."

"Minor damage," Nate said. "I may need a new suit, and Alice definitely needs a new—" he gestured to her dress and shoes "—everything."

Evie shook her head. "Since when does PR and event planning include live stunts?"

The young police officer escorted the fighter

in handcuffs through the station door, and Nate moved aside to let them pass. The man's head was down and his shoulders sagged. The door opened again and a young woman shoved her way into the police station—past Alice, Nate, June and Evie—and got in the handcuffed man's face.

"Carter, you moron, what were you doing back there? Did you think you were some kind of cowboy?"

"I didn't mean to fall off the train. I just wanted to take a solid swing at your brother. He said I was worthless and no good for you."

"So you wanted to prove him wrong by decking him?"

"Come on, Scarlet. You know I love you," Carter said.

Scarlet shook her head, stalked across the room, and sat in one of the plastic chairs lined up inside the police station's door.

"Why don't you tell your brother we're getting married," Carter continued.

"Tell him yourself," Scarlet said. She nodded toward the door where the other man entered wearing handcuffs.

"What do you have to tell me," he asked, sneering at Carter, "or would you rather use your fists, you stupid jerk? I hope you're happy. We're both in trouble, and you aren't five minutes closer to marrying my sister."

Carter bristled, and Nate thought he was going to witness part two of the unfinished fight. He wanted to tell Alice, June and Evie to move out of the range of flying fists, but Alice stepped between the two men.

"You have to believe there's a better way to resolve this," she said.

"From a jail cell?" Carter asked.

Alice turned to the police officers. "What charges are these two facing?"

The older officer shrugged. "There's some wiggle room. It's private property and we have jurisdiction to decide who goes downtown." The officer turned to both handcuffed men. "Are either of you interested in pressing assault charges?"

Carter stared at Scarlet's brother and then shook his head.

"I just want him to stay away from my sister," the other man said. "If he'll take his fists to me, I don't want to think about what could happen if she marries him."

"Who says we're still getting married?" Scarlet asked. "Maybe I changed my mind after that embarrassing brawl." She sniffed. "I'm starting to think I can do better."

Was breaking it off in a police station better than decimating a rehearsal dinner? Nate almost felt sorry for Carter, dumbass though he was.

"Is there a place where they can talk this out?" Alice asked the police officer. "Without the handcuffs?"

"Your call," the officer said. "There's a room right there, but I'll stand outside the door just in case."

He uncuffed both men and walked them to the break room. "You sure about this?" he asked Alice.

She nodded and followed the two men and Scarlet inside. Against his better judgment, which said *don't get involved*, Nate walked into the room and pressed himself flat against the wall. This was outside his job description. Way outside. But maybe he could find a way to control the narrative if he listened in.

"If anyone should be pressing charges," Alice said, pacing back and forth in front of the table where Scarlet sat with her brother and her potential fiancé, "it's me. You made a hot mess out of a wedding I spent weeks planning. My dress is ruined, I lost the heel off my shoe, and as far as I know, the bride is sobbing in her champagne because a fight broke out on her special day."

The two men looked down, chagrined.

"And no matter how lousy my day is, yours is worse," Alice said.

Nate kept his position on the wall, wondering where Alice was going with this and why she was sticking her nose in someone else's business.

"Sure is," Carter said. "My stupid temper."

Alice stopped pacing and stood in front of him. "Is her brother right? Would you ever hurt Scarlet if you were angry?"

"No," he said. He got to his feet. "I just don't like people telling me I'm no good. Like he'd know."

"What does he know about you?"

"Not much."

"Do you think that may be the problem?" Alice asked.

Scarlet raised her head and looked interested in the conversation for the first time. "Do you think these two could hug each other and become drinking buddies? You must have hit your head when you fell off that train."

"I actually jumped off the train because I didn't want to leave you by yourself," Alice said to Carter. "And I can still go out there and ask the police officers to press charges, or you two can face up to your problems."

"You mean shake hands and let it go?" the brother asked.

"No. I mean actually face it. Talk to each other. Carter, you need some anger counseling. And Scarlet, you and Carter both need couples counseling if you're really thinking about getting married."

Her brother snorted.

"You're not an innocent party here," Alice told him.

He looked back at the floor.

Nate was impressed. Not only was Alice trying to defuse the situation and offer three troubled people suggestions for help, she was doing it with half a dress and one working shoe. What would have happened if she'd forced an honest conversation with him five years ago instead of just walking away at the rehearsal dinner and shutting him out?

An hour later, the three people involved in

the fight left the police station without facing charges and with preliminary appointments with a therapist in Bayside who could help them. At June's suggestion, Alice went over to wardrobe to get a dress and shoes from the large stock of clothes on hand there. Nate waited for her outside, and they shared a ride in the police car to the reception tent by the Wonderful West train station.

"They didn't have pink?" Nate asked as they rode in the back seat. He gestured at Alice's navy blue dress and flesh-colored heels.

Alice gave him a quizzical look, her eyebrows raised. "Only in a style that doesn't work for me," she said.

She turned and gazed out the window, leaving Nate to wonder what she was thinking.

CHAPTER SIX

AFTER WORKING SEVERAL years for a giant entertainment corporation, Nate was getting used to the more intimate way things were done at Starlight Point. Being family owned, there were no shareholders to pacify. He saw one or more of the owners every day. It was friendlier, but the stakes also seemed higher because he knew the people who depended on the company's success.

There'd been events and even wedding coordinators at his previous job, but tucked away in the public relations office, he never saw them. Unless he was very careful, he would see Alice Birmingham a dozen times a day. So far, he'd tried to be careful. He hadn't seen her in the three days since the train incident, except in passing or from a distance.

It was better that way. But he couldn't avoid seeing her at tonight's management meeting. Anyone who had an office in the two-story corporate building was invited to a monthly dinner at the restaurant in the marina. Also attending were the head of maintenance, Mel Preston, who was married to June Hamilton; the head of vendor relations, Augusta Hamilton, who was Jack's wife; and Evie's husband, Scott Bennett, the fire chief at Starlight Point.

Several mid-level managers of rides, resorts, food and other services were also in attendance. Nate found his seat at one of the four tables arranged in a giant square in the marina restaurant's private banquet room. With the table arrangement, every attendee could see everyone else.

"How do you like it here?" Jack Hamilton asked as he took the chair on Nate's right. "This is your first dinner meeting, so I could give you some pointers if you want."

"Sure."

Jack cleared his throat, leaned close and said, "Have the steak."

"Is that all?" Nate asked. He'd expected a great revelation about how the meeting would go, whether he should keep his head down and his mouth shut and if there would be dessert.

Nearly all the seats around the table were full, and Nate was starting to think Alice wasn't coming. That would be for the best because ever since he'd held her close after their harrowing jump from the train, he'd felt a strange sense of the past creeping in. Maybe it was the autumn season, nostalgia abounding in the cool nights and turning leaves.

A breeze washed over his neck as the door behind him was pulled open, and he shivered. Nate realized he'd have to invest in new fall and winter clothing if he planned to stick around. After four years in Florida, he was looking forward to the change of season, but he was as unprepared for it as he'd been to face his father's failing health.

"Sorry, I was almost late," Alice said. He turned, wondering why she was apologizing to him, and then he realized she was talking to June, who was seated nearby. "I was at the florist downtown with a bride, and she had the hardest time choosing between lilies and roses."

"Were you able to help her out?" June asked.

"I think looking at the prices helped her. Lilies are way out of season for an October wedding. I had already told her that, but I think dollars and common sense spoke louder than I did."

"They usually do," June agreed. "We had red and white roses at my Christmas wedding."

"We did?" Mel asked.

June gave him a look that was part exasperation and part loving patience. "You don't remember?"

Mel shrugged. "I was busy marrying the love of my life. All I could see was you." He kissed June on the cheek.

"I wish I'd recorded that to use on our website," Nate said.

"I could provide a valuable public service to potential grooms everywhere," Mel said, grinning. "Your number one excuse for not getting too involved in the wedding planning is that you've already made the best and most important decision by choosing your bride."

A memory of Alice running over a list of plans for their wedding flashed into Nate's mind. They'd been in downtown Bayside on a bench watching the sunset right after college graduation. Alice had asked him about the colors of something…what was it? Napkins at the reception or decorations in the church?

It hadn't mattered in the end because they never made it to the reception or the church.

June flicked her napkin at her husband. "And you think that gets you guys off the hook?"

"Yes," Mel and Jack said at the same time.

"Speaking of the company website," June said, smiling at both men and giving up the battle as she focused on Nate, "I love the total refresh. It's much more colorful and interactive than it used to be, and the pictures are beautiful."

Nate cleared his throat. "Thank you." He was glad to have the conversation turned back to work topics, which seemed much safer than the marriage and happiness track it had gotten on. He had nothing to add and felt inadequate sitting there in silence waiting for dinner. Especially with Alice close enough to touch.

He glanced sideways and Alice caught him. The low light in the restaurant turned her hair to a deep rich red and Nate let his attention linger two seconds longer than he should have.

"The website has done a great job featuring

some of our recent weddings and the preparations for the fall festival weekends," Alice said.

"Keep it up, and you'll be here for life," Jack said. "And I can remind my sisters every day that it was my idea to hire you."

Did he want to be here for life? When Nate had given up his job to return to Bayside, his plans had been open-ended. He'd be here for his father's cancer treatments, reconnect with his sister and her son and then what? He hated even thinking about the end of the road for his father—would it mean restored health and no longer needing Nate, or would Nate lose his dad?

"I'm starving," Evie Hamilton declared as she stood up. She was seated across the room but spoke loudly over the two dozen people, who were all chatting. "I say we order our food first and then talk business."

"Finally," Jack said.

Restaurant staff circulated and wrote down which dinner—chicken or steak—each guest wanted. Nate went with Jack's suggestion, deferring to his wisdom and experience. He noticed Alice ordered the chicken. She'd always been a light eater except for her love of mashed potatoes and gravy. He'd been avoiding those foods as part of his plan to bury the past.

"We have some time before the food arrives," Evie said. "Our main topic for discussion tonight is the incredible success of the fall weekends. Round of applause for Alice Birmingham, our special events goddess." Everyone clapped politely and Nate joined them, feeling the eyes of the room turned toward the woman on his left but afraid to look himself. "The real test begins next weekend with the haunted houses," Evie continued. "We invested a pile of money in those, and we're hoping all the people who've come to the fall weekends so far will want to come back again for a good scare."

"I'm sure they will," Jack said. "Roller coaster fans have nerves of steel, and we're tapping into the same demographic."

A number of people nodded.

"Our PR department is also doing an excellent job," Evie continued. "Nate Graham's a one-man show taking pictures and writing articles. Our social media and print presence is really helping sell the fall weekends." She nodded and smiled at Nate and people clapped for him.

"Nice work," Alice said quietly, and he regretted not congratulating her a moment ago. Maybe it was easier for her to be brave with him because she was the one who'd called off their engagement. Were they ever going to talk about it? God, he hoped not.

"Each department head can submit estimates on staffing and expenditures to my accounting department," Evie continued. "So far, the revenue far exceeds the cost, and I like seeing those numbers. Our next order of business is the Christmas weekends. I know we're still in the planning stages, but we have a solid idea of what they'll look like. Our big question is whether or not we'll have the attendance figures for those weekends that we're seeing now."

"I think we will," someone said.

"I hope so," Evie agreed, "but there could be a foot of snow on the ground in December, and we're a summer park. It might be a challenge. We're experts at getting gum and cigarettes off the midway, not snow."

"I hope there's a foot of snow on the ground," Alice said. "That will make my ice skating rink, Christmas tree lot and sleigh rides a whole lot more fun."

"I wonder how many people will come here to skate when there's an indoor rink only an hour away," Evie said. "I love your idea, but I'm always thinking about the dollars and columns."

"The rink an hour away is nice," Alice said. "Believe me, I spent three days a week there when I was a kid. But do you know what they don't have? Roller coasters in the background. The smell of evergreens from our tree lot. Sleigh bells and fresh air."

"Good selling point," Evie replied. "Why did you spend so much time at the indoor rink?"

"Junior figure skating competitions. My sisters were soccer players, but I loved figure skating."

"It was the costumes, I'd bet," June said. "Alice is my twin when it comes to appreciating sparkle, even though she pretends to be more pragmatic."

"I did win second place for one of my costumes," Alice said, "even though the highest medal I got for my skating was third place."

"That's what counts," June said, laughing. She raised her glass to Alice in a mock toast. After that, the waitstaff delivered salads and

Evie postponed the rest of the formal business until after they enjoyed their food.

Nate tried to eat, but his consciousness of Alice right at his elbow stole his appetite. He'd forgotten about her junior figure skating days. They were over by the time they'd started dating senior year, but the trophies had been on her parents' fireplace mantel. Did she ever skate nowadays?

The more he worked with her, the more the past assailed him at every turn. Keeping his professional smile at work was twelve times more difficult with his ex-fiancée filling his radar screen.

CHAPTER SEVEN

"I'M SEEING STARLIGHT POINT with fresh eyes," Virginia told her son Jack as he stooped and picked up a candy wrapper from the midway. She'd seen her husband, Ford, do the same thing dozens of times. Her oldest looked so much like his father. Every once in a while, Virginia almost thought she was seeing her late husband when she caught a glimpse of Jack from across the midway.

"Did you get new glasses?" Jack teased.

Virginia laughed. "I never imagined staying open throughout the fall and winter because I always thought of Starlight Point as a summer resort, but now I see it's just as beautiful in the autumn."

"You and Dad were probably wiser than we are. If we stay open four more months, when am I ever going to get some rest and recharge for next year?" Jack asked.

"There's more than one way to recharge,"

Virginia said. "You could paint one of these pumpkins. Art is very therapeutic."

"Judging from the cars coming across the bridge, you're going to need all the pumpkins and paint you've got," Jack said. "After last weekend, we doubled our supplies of pumpkin pie, apple cider and even cinnamon squash ice cream."

Three hours later, Virginia realized how right her son was. She and Henry worked side by side handing out pumpkins, distributing art supplies and even helping kids glue yarn wigs on their creations. The line at their craft station next to the kiddieland carousel wasn't dwindling, but their supplies were.

"We may get desperate here and just hand out carving knives to the kids," Henry said.

Virginia laughed. "I called Alice and asked her to send more paint, yarn and glue." She pointed toward the kiddieland carousel. "Here she comes."

Alice threaded her way through the crowd but stopped to admire a little girl's artistic creation, taking a moment to snap a picture of the girl and her mother with the mother's smartphone. Virginia imagined that photo would be a keeper, worthy of being printed and framed. Her house was still full of those reminders of her children and her husband. Even though she lived alone, she had their smiling faces frozen in time to keep her company.

"Your hands are empty," Henry said when Alice approached. "Do you need me to go haul boxes of supplies?"

"Not exactly," Alice said as she draped an arm around both Virginia and Henry and pulled them aside. "I checked our storage area, and we're cleaned out of pumpkin craft items."

"Uh-oh," Virginia said, eyeing the line of wiggly children. "At this rate, I would estimate we have two hours' worth of supplies left. Maybe less."

"So we go with carving knives?" Henry asked.

"No," Virginia and Alice said together.

"I'll be glad to go on an emergency supply run," Henry offered. "My car is in the marina lot and I could try to hustle back before the kids paint through what we have left."

"Would you?" Alice asked.

"Sure. Just tell me where to get art supplies in Bayside."

"There's a craft superstore on the west side of town, just beyond where they built the train overpass a few years ago," Virginia said.

She'd been there with her girlfriends on one of their lunch outings. The store had only been open a year, but it was already a favorite because they had yarn in every color and texture imaginable, home decor and candles. There was even a classroom in the back where she and her friends had attempted to make a holiday wreath out of foam and ribbons. Her final product hadn't looked much like the sample, but the instructor had said it was the thought that counted. Virginia had raised a glass of wine afterward with her friends, toasting their artistic attempts.

"They built a train overpass?" Henry asked.

"How long have you been away?" Alice replied, smiling.

"Since I was old enough to enlist in the air force. But don't worry, I'll find the store if you give me good directions. There used to be a great place to get ice cream on the west side. I wonder if it's still there?"

"I remember it," Virginia said. "My sister

and I used to ride our bikes there when we got our babysitting money in the summer. The scoops always overflowed the cone and we'd have to ride home with sticky hands." She also remembered taking her own children there with her husband at the wheel of the family car. He'd never minded a few ice cream drips on the car's seats.

Alice and Virginia described the rerouted state highway and the location of the craft superstore. Henry wrote directions on the back of a live shows program Virginia found on the midway, and he also wrote down the list of supplies both women suggested.

As he tucked the paper in his shirt pocket, he turned to Alice. "Do you think you could find replacements for me *and* Virginia for the next two hours?"

At Henry's words, Virginia felt a lightness in her chest as if she were one of the many seagulls taking off from the beach in front of the hotel. Was he going to suggest they go together? Her past memories of Ford and her present friendship with Henry blended in a watery mixture she couldn't separate.

"Sure," Alice said. Did she have to sound so eager? Her willingness to help was clearly going to lead to a tough choice for Virginia, and she'd already made so many in the five years since Ford had passed away quietly on a park bench at Starlight Point without getting a chance to say goodbye.

"I was thinking," Henry said, turning a wide smile on Virginia. She knew what was coming. "If you came along and made sure I didn't get lost, we'd save enough time to stop and see if that ice cream place is still there."

Virginia knew full well that it was, because she'd driven by it dozens of times over the years. Did she want to open her trove of memories and layer Henry over parts of them?

"I shouldn't," she said, shaking her head. "I'd feel bad leaving when there's so much work to do." Blaming her refusal on work was a safe excuse, even though it was cowardly.

Henry held out a hand. "Come with me. I need a copilot."

Virginia hesitated, torn between feeling like a girl being asked on a date and a woman turning her back on her past.

Alice laughed suddenly, intruding on Virginia's thoughts. "It's just shopping and ice cream, Virginia. You'll be back before the paint dries on these pumpkins, and I'd feel better sending you to the craft store to make sure Henry gets the washable paint. We don't want parents to hate us."

"When you put it that way, I guess I better go along," Virginia said. She joined Henry and walked by his side toward the marina gate, but she didn't take his hand. She needed to keep things in perspective.

"I WOULDN'T ASK if I wasn't desperate," Alice said, grabbing Nate's shirtsleeve as he took a picture of the pumpkins lined up on her table. She leaned close and the movement caught him by surprise. Their heads knocked together and they both laughed and rubbed their foreheads. Nate drew back quickly and his smile returned to neutral.

"What's the emergency?" he asked.

"I'm fighting the battle of the pumpkin station and losing. I sent Virginia and Henry off for supplies an hour ago, but I haven't found anyone to replace them."

"I'm sure they'll be back soon," Nate said.

"Not soon enough," Alice replied, pointing down the long line of kids waiting for their turn at the pumpkin decorating station.

Parents juggled strollers, bags and toddlers. Their faces suggested the patience that comes with parenthood, but how long could it last?

"If you're out of supplies, I'm not sure what you want me to do," Nate said.

Was he really refusing to offer ideas or lend a hand? Alice remembered a different Nate from their high school days. He'd gotten a good citizenship award and had been a member of the school honor society. He was the kind of guy a teacher would ask to deliver a note to the office or show a new kid around.

But only Alice knew that his affability was an outside layer, always protecting a deep center he never let anyone see. Even her, the woman he'd asked to be his wife and share his future. How much of that life would she have shared if she'd gone through with the marriage? She didn't know, and that was what had scared her out of the wedding at the last minute.

Alice swallowed and reminded herself their job was not about their past or what they had shared. It was about making Starlight Point a success. And at the moment, success meant making kids and parents happy by helping them decorate pumpkins. She offered

Nate a professional smile. "We're not totally out. Help me with this? Please?"

Nate sighed and put his camera on a box behind Alice's table. "I'll get another table from the storage room behind the ballroom and get someone to help me haul some chairs over here. That way it'll at least look like we're accommodating more people."

"I hope to more than just *look* like we're doing our jobs," Alice said. Did it always have to be about appearances with him?

"Do you want the chairs and tables or not?"

She pressed her lips together and cut a glance to the waiting kids. "Fine. Yes. Please."

"I'll be right back."

As promised, Nate hauled a long table to a spot next to Alice's and had it on its feet only five minutes later. Three maintenance men juggling two chairs under each arm followed him. As a dozen children sat up to the table and reached for their pie-sized pumpkins, the line flexed and settled.

"Nice work," Alice said. "Thank you."

"Just avoiding a riot," Nate answered.

Alice laughed. "I'm trying to picture a riot involving strollers and sippy cups."

"They're the worst. Those parents are armed with enough supplies to withstand a siege, and little kids are usually five minutes from a meltdown."

"How do you know all this?" Alice asked. It had never occurred to her that Nate might have moved on, even had a child or two of his own in the past five years. Silence had been a wall between them.

"My sister has three-year-old twins. Those last few minutes before naptime or bedtime are a minefield of emotion."

How many men refer to emotion as a mine-field?

"So you don't babysit much," she commented as they stood shoulder to shoulder watching parents help their kids transform pumpkins into art.

"You know I've been working in Florida."

Alice nodded. She swallowed, wanting to ask about his reasons for coming home. She'd heard through the company grapevine about his father's illness. She remembered Mr. Graham, of course. How many times had she been at Nate's house during high school and then their two-year engagement? She could picture Murray Graham's face at the rehearsal dinner when she finally got up the courage to face the fact she wasn't ready to marry his son.

"How was Florida?" she asked, trying to forget the image of Nate's father's stricken face. When she'd replayed her bombshell moment later, she remembered that Nate's father had shown a bigger reaction than the jilted man himself.

"Fine," Nate said. "Florida is very hot, and the crowds in the amusement park there make this look like a private party."

"Did you miss home?"

"Sometimes."

Was she one of the things he'd missed? She doubted it. She risked a glance but found his face was a mask of PR diplomacy. Anyone passing by would think they were talking about the weather or why leaves change colors in the fall.

Alice was tired of dodging her past. Their past.

"I'm sorry about your father's illness."

"Thank you," he said coldly.

"It's kind of you to come home and help him through this."

"I'm his son."

This was even harder than she'd imagined, even though she knew Nate was capable of bricking up a wall in record time if emotion was on the other side.

"Well, I wish…I mean…if there's anything I can do to help, I hope you'll—"

"There's nothing I need from you, Alice."

Alice crossed her arms and turned away, his cold words leaving a trail of ice through her stomach. *Was that how married life would have been whenever a tough subject came up?*

She sighed with relief when she saw Virginia and Henry headed toward her. They pulled a wagon filled with boxes, bags and extra pumpkins. Each of them had a hand on the wagon handle and shared the weight as they trudged down the midway. They were laughing about something, and Alice imagined they could have pulled that wagon all the way to the Wonderful West without noticing any burden.

If only Nate would let me share some of the weight of his problems, she thought. She turned to him with the intention of being more direct with her offer. They were once engaged…

Instead of getting a chance, she got a view of his back as he strode toward the older couple and took the handle from Virginia. He gave Virginia a warm smile and clapped Henry on the back.

Nate was perfectly capable of being nice to other people, but Alice wondered what would happen if they tried to get too close to him. And what about his father's illness? Did he wear his neutral mask sitting by his father's side during chemotherapy?

CHAPTER EIGHT

HENRY DROPPED OFF a big box of pamphlets he'd picked up from the printer in Bayside. "We should set up our own print shop here at Starlight Point instead of outsourcing it," he said. "It seems like it would save money and time."

Nate looked up from his computer. "I could suggest it to one of the Hamiltons, but I'd guess there's probably a reason they do it this way. Maybe it's good that the Point has connections with local businesses."

"Unless it's a project that requires secrecy," Henry commented. "The lady at the print shop almost talked my ear off about the fall festivals, and she wanted to know what the Christmas events would be like. I told her I was only the errand boy and I didn't know a thing. I hardly made it out of there."

Nate smiled as he got up and opened the box. He took out a glossy brochure and admired it. Just like the proofs he'd approved, the warm fall colors and enticing photography and fonts made the upcoming October weekends so appealing anyone would want to visit—even those who'd already been there in September. "Maybe she liked you," he told Henry.

Henry chuckled. "I don't think that's a likely explanation. How about you? I'd hate to see a young man like you make the mistakes I did and end up alone."

"You don't seem that lonely to me. What mistakes are you talking about?"

"I always thought I was too busy to have a wife, and I wasn't so sure any woman would want me anyway."

"Why not?"

Henry shrugged. "I used to think I should be in charge of everything. Not that I was bossy, I just wanted control so I could make sure things went the way I thought they should."

"A good trait for a pilot."

"Maybe. These days, I've learned to sit back and let someone else take the lead."

"So maybe it's not too late for you," Nate suggested lightly, hoping to shrug off the conversation. He didn't want to get into a discussion on his love life. To his amazement, no one at the Point seemed to know he and Alice had once been engaged. It was far better to keep it that way. Explanations would unquestionably be a messy dive into the past that neither of them wanted or needed. Not that he could predict her emotions. He'd obviously never been good at that. He'd loved her, and he'd truly believed she felt the same until she chose the most public way to embarrass him and reject him.

"I think you should ask out one of the pretty girls around here. How about Alice? Virginia said you two might have already known each other."

The shiny brochures slid out of Nate's hands and spread in a colorful wave on his office floor. What had Henry heard or seen that would make him say that? "Definitely not."

Henry didn't comment, but he raised both eyebrows at Nate's tone of finality. He knelt and helped Nate scoop up the glossy papers.

"I'm working on some of the HTML for our company website," Nate said as he stacked the pamphlets neatly in the box. Writing code—where he was in complete command of what the computer did—was a much safer choice than discussing his feelings with Henry. Or anyone.

"I don't know what that means, but it sounds important."

"I think so. When I took this job, I asked who was in charge of the website, and I got a vague answer, so I decided to take charge of it. If I make some improvements now and launch it this winter, it will make our web presence a lot stronger for next year's season."

"I'm already looking forward to next summer," Henry observed.

Nate wondered what it would be like to stay here next year, and the next. What were Alice's plans? Would she stay at Starlight Point, as well?

When he was young and had asked her to marry him in an unexpected surge of emotions, he'd wanted them to grow old together. Whatever that looked like. His mother's death when he was twelve robbed him of his chance to see his parents do just that. Would he accidentally end up by Alice's side for life, working at Starlight Point?

A large chocolate lab with shiny fur and big brown eyes poked its head through Nate's door. The dog wore a collar, but a long purple leash dragged on the ground.

"Gladys," Henry said. "Where did you lose your owner?"

"You know this dog?"

Henry nodded. "Virginia's. She sprung her from the humane society at the end of the summer." He got up and rubbed an affectionate hand over the dog's head. He picked up the leash and leaned into the hallway. "Virginia?" he called.

"In June's office," Virginia answered from down the hall.

"I've got Gladys."

"I knew she wouldn't get far. Be right there."

Henry stood at Nate's door with the leash looped around his hand. Gladys sat and wagged her tail as Nate approached and put out his hand to shake one of the dog's long slender paws. "I like dogs," he said. "They're not complicated."

"You should get one. Might be good therapy for your dad, too."

Nate considered the idea. He hadn't had a

pet in years. His mother had a cat that out-lived her by a few years. He remembered his father and sister sobbing when Beatrice had died... It had been like reliving his mother's death.

He wasn't ready for a cat. But a dog? Alice was a dog person. Her family had two dogs when they'd dated. Did they still have those dogs? Five years was a long time in the life of a human, but almost half a lifetime for dogs. He wanted to ask Alice if those match-ing beagles still slept behind the couch in her parents' living room. What were their names? Hector and...the memory escaped him.

Virginia appeared in the doorway. "We were just going home to take a walk on the beach," she said.

"It's a beautiful evening. I was thinking of microwaving a chicken pot pie and eating it on my porch," Henry said. He handed the leash to Virginia, who ran it through her fin-gers as if she was thinking about something.

"I have frozen dinners and a porch," Vir-ginia said. "And Gladys likes your company."

Henry put a hand on the dog's head. "I feel the same way about her."

They walked down the hall together and June came by a moment later.

"Did you just see that?" she asked Nate.

"I'm not sure what I saw."

"I think I saw my mother going on a date."

Nate smiled. "I heard something about chicken pot pie and a porch. I don't know what you're talking about."

June rolled her eyes and knocked on the door across the hall. "You in there, Alice?"

To his surprise, Alice gave a muffled response. He hadn't realized she'd been right there while he talked to Henry with his office door open. Even if she had listened in, which he doubted, she wouldn't have heard anything she didn't already know.

"My mother wasn't very sympathetic," June said, dropping into Alice's chair. "I don't think she remembers what it was like when we were all little and Dad worked late. Sometimes I look at the clock and count the hours until bath and bedtime."

"How old is Abigail?" Alice asked.

"One and a half. She'll be two in January."

"That sounds like a fun age. One of my

sisters who has little kids says the days are long but the years are short."

"You have two sisters?" June asked.

Alice nodded. "One married and one semi-engaged."

"You've probably heard Evie is pregnant. It will be nice to share the chaos of motherhood with her. For her sake, I hope Scott helps out a lot, especially during the operating season."

"Does Mel often work late?"

"Two nights a week during the summer, same as me. We're trading back and forth on these fall weekends."

"Do you think he looks at the clock and counts the hours until bath and bedtime on those nights when you work late?" Alice asked.

June wrinkled her nose. "I see what you're doing."

Alice leaned back in her padded desk chair and crossed one leg over the other. "I was just asking a question, trying to establish the facts."

"Complaining is more fun."

"Tell me about the Halloween-themed show you're getting ready for the Midway Theater," Alice said.

"You're changing the subject before I get around to asking why a gorgeous single girl like you is unattached."

"What kind of show was that again?" Alice asked with a smile. The last thing she wanted to do was admit she was once engaged to the man who occupied the office across the hall. June was a friend, but it was too raw, even after five years. She'd put those feelings in storage, but Nate showing up had opened the box.

"Fun stuff," June said. "Classic horror movie soundtracks and monster-themed songs. I had to beg Gloria to make us some new costume pieces, even though we tried to reuse some of the summer ones. We added orange vests and masquerade masks. A few top hats decked out with bats and spider-webs."

"Will those be hard to dance in?"

"Not for my performers. They're used to costumes and crowds after singing and dancing all summer here. Some of them had to wear the moon and stars on their heads when they danced in the daily parade. I'm just lucky I got enough of them to come back for fall weekends to put on a show."

"People will love it," Alice said. "And the shows will be popular with guests who hate haunted houses."

"And kids. It's family-rated," June said. "I had Ross preview it and he declared it—" June paused and used air quotes "—way not scary. He's nine, he would know."

"I love Ross," Alice said. "He's cute and funny, and he looks just like a miniature version of his dad."

June nodded. "He's from Mel's first marriage. She was a performer here at the Point who didn't stick around."

"Did they get married here?" Alice had guessed that June and Mel were a second-chance romance because June had mentioned a long hiatus in their relationship, but she hadn't asked details about how they got together.

"No, in Bayside. Mel's mother showed me a picture once, even though Mel didn't keep any evidence."

Alice thought of the pictures her mother had snapped of her trying on her wedding dress. Those pictures were in a shoebox in her parents' attic along with pictures of Nate she collected during their two-year relationship.

There was a picture of the two of them at Starlight Point, taken on a sunny Saturday after they'd graduated from high school. He'd dared her to ride the Silver Streak, and she'd taken the challenge by getting on the coaster five times in a row. Her hair was wild and windblown in the picture and she had a reckless smile. When she tried to remember Nate's smile in the photo, she could only picture the dispassionate one she'd grown accustomed to. Was it always that way?

"They were married for about five minutes, I guess," June continued.

"I hate when marriages go bad, especially after all the money and effort people put into the ceremony." Alice sighed. "I always hope for happy endings."

She thought of her expensive wedding dress her father had worked overtime to pay for. It still hung in the closet of the spare bedroom at her parents' house. Every time her parents hosted out of town guests, Alice quietly moved it to the back of her own closet. At least it only happened once a year or so. And it wouldn't be long now before she paid her parents back. It was going to feel so good.

"Mel got a happy ending, the second time

around," June said. "I'm the one he should have married in the first place, but we were too young to know that." June took a mint from a bowl on Alice's desk and unwrapped it. The clear cellophane wrapper crackled loudly in the quiet office. Nearly everyone else had gone home for the day.

Someone knocked on Alice's office door and she called, "Come in."

"Sorry to bother you," Nate said as he stuck his head in her office. "I just wanted to ask you something."

"Okay," Alice said. So far, Nate had only voluntarily entered her office when he got the wrong sandwich. And that was only once. This had to be an important business matter.

Nate looked at June and then back at Alice. "It's about your dogs. The beagles."

Had the floor opened up and delivered her into another dimension? Nate was bringing up a personal subject—with a witness?

"I was trying to remember their names. Hector and…?"

"Homer," Alice said, completely befuddled but her tongue quickly supplying the answer. The two dogs had been inseparable all their lives. Even their names went together.

Nate nodded. "Hector and Homer. That's right. Are they…?"

Alice shook her head. "They were getting old when we were—I mean, they were getting up there in age. They passed away a year or two ago."

"Oh," Nate said. "Sorry. I was talking to Henry about dogs and I—well, I should go."

He backed away and pulled the door shut. His footsteps moved quickly down the hallway as if he were practically running.

Alice turned and opened a window to let the cool autumn air fan her cheeks. When she turned back around, June was staring at her as if she'd never seen her before.

Instead of commenting, Alice sliced open a box of wedding samples on a table near her desk and started pulling them out. "This engraved one is gorgeous, but it has to be really expensive," she said. "Still, there might be some brides who—"

"Start talking," June said.

"I am."

"About the dogs."

"Hector and Homer were from the same litter," Alice said evenly. Her mind raced but she paced her words. "My aunt found them in the woods near her house and we adopted them when I was about ten. My sister was reading some book about mythology at the time and she named them."

"And Nate knows about them how?"

"Everyone knows about Greek mythology."

"I mean the beagles."

"He's from Bayside," Alice said, hoping the explanation would be enough.

"Did he live next door to you or date one of your sisters?"

"No."

"Was he a professional dog walker during high school?" June asked.

"Would you believe me if I said yes?"

"No."

"Nate and I used to…know each other."

"In high school?"

"And after," Alice said. "But we went our separate ways then, and we like to keep our past and present separate now."

"Which is why he was just in here trying to remember the names of your family dogs."

Alice's heart fell down an elevator shaft in her body. "I have no idea what brought that on. Maybe it was seeing your mother's dog."

June swished her lips to the side in a skeptical slant. "Sure. My mother's chocolate lab Gladys would remind anyone of two beagles named Hector and Homer."

Alice nodded. "Only explanation I can think of," she said. But what *was* the reason Nate was digging around in the past?

CHAPTER NINE

THE WEDDING ON the first Friday of October had two potential locations depending upon the weather. Alice had the ballroom reserved, but the bride truly wanted the wedding to take place at the midway carousel. Because her father was the publisher of the *Bayside Times* and several other newspapers in Michigan, his money was squarely behind whatever his daughter wanted.

"I think he bought off the weather gods," Alice told Haley. "When is it sunny and seventy degrees in October?"

"Today," Haley said. She picked up one end of a roll of white carpet runner. "This is as heavy as wet laundry."

"I'll help," Henry said. "You hold it down, and I'll unroll it."

Alice placed name cards on the rows of white chairs while Henry carefully unrolled and smoothed the white runner. The midway had been swept clean by the grounds crew, and Alice and her decorators showed up early as soon as they were certain of sunny skies.

"How many people are invited?" Henry asked.

"A million," Haley said.

Alice laughed. "Two hundred. But more for the reception. I'm only labeling the first five rows of chairs on both sides of the aisle, and the rest of the guests can decide for themselves where to sit."

Each of the place cards matched the wedding's carousel theme, including ornately painted horses. The bridesmaids would wear jewel-toned dresses, and the carousel would be in operation while the guests found their seats. *Pure magic.* The bride had told Alice she wanted her wedding guests to remember the event the rest of their lives.

"Never get tired of carousel music," Henry said.

"Gotta be kidding me," Haley grumbled. "How long have you worked here?"

Henry shrugged. "All summer."

Haley shoved her dark hair back from her face. "I've worked here all summer, too, and I'm thinking of unplugging that stupid organ."

Alice stopped taping deep blue, red and purple bows on the sides of the chairs along the aisle and straightened up.

"You're not going to like this," she told Haley. "The bride's father didn't pay the usual fee to have a wedding at Starlight Point. Instead, he pledged a lot of money to have the carousel restored."

"You're kidding."

"Not at all. Horses will be repainted in their original 1920s colors, motor rebuilt, and—the best part—the original Wurlitzer organ will be louder and more beautiful than ever if you come back next summer."

Haley crossed her arms over her chest. "I think I'll get a job at Disneyland instead."

"They have a carousel," Henry said. "I flew out of Anaheim a few thousand times."

"But everything else at Disneyland is so loud you won't be able to hear the carousel," Haley said.

"You may have a point there," Henry agreed. He turned to Alice. "Why the big deal with the carousel?"

"It's a father-daughter thing from what I

understand. I guess they loved to come here in the summer and ride this carousel—and the one in the Wonderful West—over and over. The father of the bride is also on a museum board and has connections with artists who restore these national treasures." Alice emphasized the last two words while grinning at Haley, who rolled her eyes.

"Is it too late to hope for rain?"

"Yes," Alice said. "This will be the wedding of the year so far. After the ceremony, the bridal party and guests get a ride on the carousel, and then everyone troops down the midway to the ballroom for a champagne lunch with a live band. It may not be the wedding of *your* dreams, but it's a dream wedding for the bride and that's what counts."

"It's going to be a long day," Haley said. "The haunted houses open tonight, and I'm planning to go through them if I still have any energy after this wedding."

"You'll have time for a nap," Alice assured her. "The wedding reception ends late afternoon, and the haunted houses don't open until almost dark."

Haley sighed and opened one of the long white boxes the florist had delivered just an hour before. She pulled out a garland of fresh roses wound around a green wire. The red roses were complimented by gold and jewel-toned ribbons.

"Lucky for us," Alice continued. "The grounds crew already removed the skeletons and other Halloween decorations from the carousel. They'll put them back later today. For now, all you have to do is drape one of those garlands around the necks of all the horses on the outside row."

"Like they've just won the Kentucky Derby," Henry announced. "That would be quite a feat in their case."

"Okay, I officially give up being grumpy about the carousel," Haley said. "This is so over-the-top that I'm starting to like it."

"I feel the same way," Alice said. "I doubt I'll top this one anytime soon."

As Haley festooned the horses with rose garlands, Henry helped Alice with the rest of the setup. At the metal railing where guests usually waited in line for the carousel, they placed heavy urns and filled them with flowers.

"The wedding pictures will be beautiful," Alice said as she used her hand to frame a shot with the flowered urns and carousel in the background.

A group of people walked into her view of the carousel. Two of them had their cell phones out and were taking pictures.

"Hello," Alice said. Of the four people, the only one she knew was Nate. Who was he showing around just hours before a huge wedding?

Nate approached her and his guests followed. "These are friends of the bride's father." He introduced the two men and a woman. "From the National Carousel Association."

"Nice to meet you," Alice said, shaking hands and trying to remember their names.

"So this is it," Nate said, sweeping his hand toward the old-fashioned carousel. "Is it worth a massive restoration?"

"Any functioning carousel from the golden age of American merry-go-rounds is worthwhile," the woman said. "And this one is a beauty. Jack Hamilton told us that aside from fresh paint on the saddles every year and new lightbulbs, it's pretty much original." Her attention shifted to the rows of white chairs and flowered urns. "We're invited to the wedding today, too. Isn't it a wonderful idea to have it here?"

"Wonderful," Alice agreed.

"What a fun job you have," the woman continued. "I would just love to go to wedding after wedding and see the dresses and cakes and decorations. Maybe I missed my calling."

"It's never too late," Alice said. "And if you love weddings, you could always have a ceremony of your own and renew your vows."

The woman laughed. "Too risky. I'm afraid if my husband got a second chance to say yes or no, he might leave me at the altar."

Alice laughed politely with the others, but the words were a dark cloud in the otherwise sunny sky.

ON SATURDAY MORNING, Nate was the first one up. He tiptoed down the steps so he wouldn't wake his dad and found the *Bayside Times*, folded and on the front porch. Nate stood outside on the peaceful morning and studied the front page, where the carousel wedding and story dominated above the fold. There was a picture of the wedding party in front of the carousel and a picture of the bride's father—the publisher of the newspaper—with his friends from the museum association. The article devoted a few paragraphs to the pledge for restoration funds...but not before reporting every minute detail of the wedding. The flowers, the bride's dress—organdy in some color called blush with a sequined cathedral train—the names of the bridal party, the food highlights from the reception and Alice's name listed as the wedding planner were in black and white for all to see.

There was also a crisp picture of Alice helping the bride onto a carousel horse. Her face was clearly visible and her smile radiant. Anyone who had ever known Alice would recognize her. Would his father?

Nate took the paper into the kitchen and discovered a dusty cardboard box on the table. A photo album lay open in front of his father's chair and pictures were scattered over the worn wooden surface where his family had eaten so many meals. He could still smell and taste his mother's cooking, remembered the pot roast and homemade macaroni and cheese. Those recipes, like her voice waking him up for school, had disappeared in the five seconds it had taken for the drunk driver to lose control.

His teen years had been takeout and frozen pizza instead of casseroles hot from the oven, and he wasn't doing much better cooking for himself and his dad. Maybe he could try harder.

"You're up early," his father said as he shuffled into the kitchen in a loose robe and slippers.

"Work," Nate said. "You must have done this late last night after I went to bed." He gestured toward the old box. "If you wanted things from the attic, I would have gotten them out for you."

Not that he wanted to. If those memories could stay tucked at the top of a narrow staircase and hidden behind cobwebs, he would prefer it. He carefully avoided looking too closely at any of the photographs.

"Didn't want to be a pain in the neck," his father said. "Bad enough you gave up your life to move home."

"I only gave up Florida," Nate said, smiling. "Not my life. It was too hot anyway, the tourist traffic was a nightmare and the spiders were huge."

His father sat while Nate pulled a loaf of bread from the cabinet and dropped four slices in the toaster.

"Thanks, son."

"Butter and jelly?"

"Yes, but I wasn't talking about the toast."

Nate gingerly moved aside photos of his family to make room for breakfast. He put the box on the empty chair where his mother used to sit and his eyes accidentally fell on a photograph of him and his sister on the kids' helicopter ride at Starlight Point.

He closed his eyes while he sealed the top flaps of the box, trying to keep his emotions in check. He was accustomed to some family pictures, including the smiling ones of his mother on the mantel and on his father's bedroom dresser. Looking at those made him feel as if time had stopped before his mother died. But it hadn't. He'd lost his mom too soon, and now he was faced with daily reminders that his dad wouldn't be here forever.

The only recent photograph in the house was a framed wedding photo of Nate's sister and their father on her wedding day. It sat opposite a lamp on a table in the living room. If

Nate and Alice had gotten married, he imagined their photo would be on that table, too.

"I was looking through these things because I'm cleaning out stuff around here," his father said. "One of my old coworkers died a year ago and his kids had a hell of a time figuring out what to do with his lifetime's accumulation. I don't want to burden you and Susan like that."

"Not a burden, Dad." Nate filled the coffee maker and hit the power button. "What time is your appointment on Monday?"

"One o'clock," his father said. "What's this?"

Nate turned around. His dad was holding the *Bayside Times* and staring at it, forehead wrinkled as if he were thinking about something puzzling.

"A wedding we had yesterday at the Point," Nate said. He leaned and pointed at the photo of the wedding party, hoping his father wouldn't see the other prominent picture in which Alice was visible.

"Were you there?"

"Of course. It's my job to publicize anything good that happens at Starlight Point."

His father put his finger on the picture of

Alice. "Don't we know this girl?" He dug his reading glasses out of the chest pocket of his robe and Nate dreaded what was coming next.

"It's Alice Birmingham," he said, hoping to avoid an emotional outburst. He'd purposely used her name instead of a descriptor. Girlfriend, fiancée, former fiancée…they were all too personal.

"Oh, son," Murray said, sadness in his voice instead of surprise or anger at the woman who'd humiliated his son. "Do you have to work with her every day? Is that what you have to put up with at your job?"

The coffeepot gurgled loudly and the toast popped up. Nate turned his back to his father. "You make it sound far more dramatic than it is."

"This damn cancer," his father said. "I wish you didn't have to suffer, too."

"I'm not suffering. I love my job, and seeing Alice once in a while is a small price to pay for getting to watch the sunsets over the lake and get fresh coffee from the lobby of the Lake Breeze Hotel every day."

"Are you sure?" his father asked.

Nate gave his father a practiced smile. "Of course I'm sure."

CHAPTER TEN

ON SATURDAY EVENING, an hour before the spooky Wonderful West carousel and the haunted house in the shooting gallery opened to Starlight Point guests, employees were invited to go through them without battling the crowds. Alice thought the staff should have firsthand knowledge of the haunted house so they could answer guests' questions.

Looking around at everyone gathered in the Wonderful West, she was pleased to see so many off-duty employees had shown up for their chance to experience the frights without waiting in a long line. Because the haunted houses were her idea, she had to do it, too, as a show of good faith. It wasn't even dark outside, but Alice shivered just thinking about going through them.

"You're not scared, are you?" Haley asked.

"Of course I am. We hired professional scarers to put these together, remember?"

"I wonder how you get a job as a professional scarer?" Haley asked, grinning and using air quotes on the made-up word. "Probably be a psych major in college so you know how to dig around in peoples' brains and find the really terrifying stuff."

Alice zipped up her jacket and buttoned the cuffs. "Or you dig around in your own life and magnify the stuff that scares you."

Haley shuddered. "Not going there."

The door to the Western Arcade and shooting gallery opened and the doorman ushered in the next group of eight. A couple dozen people stood in line ahead of her and Haley, which gave Alice time to get even more nervous. It was a cool evening with the feeling of fall. Leaves swirled at her feet and the breeze off the lake carried the scent of cold water.

A moment later, the breeze was blocked and replaced by a warm body right behind her. She didn't turn around to see who it was, but the air changed and was spiced with a familiar smell. It was some sort of shower soap that smelled like the forest. Damp forest, but not moldy. She'd been trying to come up with a name for it for weeks.

"Hey, Nate," Haley said. "Ready to scare yourself to death?"

"Ready to let the professionals scare me," he said, his words so close that Alice almost felt his breath on her neck. "I heard we hired the best."

She turned and found herself almost close enough to touch him, although hardly nose to nose since he was a foot taller. He wore a dark green jacket and jeans, and he almost blended into the darkness, but Alice felt she would have recognized him anywhere.

"I'm not so sure about this," Haley said. "I may go back to the office and dig gum off the bottom of the trash can. I've been meaning to get that done all summer."

Alice laughed. "You're staying and suffering with the rest of us."

"As long as someone holds hands with me," Haley said.

They waited in silence for two more groups to enter the haunted house ahead of them. The plans Alice had seen showed an Old West–themed fright zone with cowboy skeletons, tombstones and bloody ranch hands. How scary could those be? But she'd seen groups of eight enter the house, then come around the corner from the back of the attraction clutching their chests and laughing nervously—and only half the group got back in line. That was *probably* a good sign.

"Next eight victims," the man at the door announced. He was dressed all in black with skeleton face paint and a black cowboy hat, and he intoned his words as if they were all truly going to their deaths.

Nice acting.

In addition to Haley and Nate, Alice's group included a handful of seasonal employees she knew only by sight. Their group inched into the haunted house and Alice's heart was racing long before the first ghastly figure lunged at their group with creepy hands and dreadful sounds. Was she really prepared for this?

"I think I'm about to pass out," Haley said. She grabbed Alice's arm and cringed against her. Nate was so close behind them he bumped into them when they slowed down or hesitated. Alice tried to be brave for Haley's sake, and because she wanted to build a reputation as someone who did not back down even in the face of adversity. Weddings could be almost as frightening as ghosts and zombies.

Alice steeled her nerves, remembering a haunted farm and hayride she'd survived back in high school. She'd gone with a group that included Nate, but it was before they'd officially dated. Back then, he'd been the quiet boy in her study hall. Her entire group had been holding hands out of fear. She'd held Nate's hand and a rush of feelings swept her through the haunted house. Having him next to her years later was a cruel irony.

A woman near her screamed and forced Alice's thoughts back to the present. Her group moved through an Old West hotel with cobwebs and flickering lights in the corridor. Numbered doors were nailed shut but straining against their boards with hideous creaking sounds as if something could jump out at any moment. A man with an ax loomed at the end of the hall and mirrors and strobe lights made him seem terrifyingly huge and close. Alice and Haley screamed at the same time and Haley's grip on her arm tightened. Someone took Alice's free hand and held on.

She knew the rules of haunted houses. *They can't touch you even though they can scare you to death.* Whoever had her hand was not with the fright crew. The hand was large and warm. In a flash of strobe light, Alice risked a glance to her left. Nate stared grimly ahead as if facing his worst nightmare—and he had a tight grip on her hand.

"Step right up to the slaughterhouse," their ghastly tour guide said. Leaving them no choice, he opened the door into a terrifying scene of butchers swinging saws and knives. Chains rattled and mixed with the horrible sounds.

"This is too much," Nate said. "I'm closing my eyes and following you. Don't let go."

"It's not real, it's not real, it's not real," Alice repeated. "Haley, it's not real, okay?"

Haley was nearly hyperventilating, only taking a break from breathing long enough to scream intermittently.

The three of them clung together and shoved through the slaughterhouse with the rest of their group. In the next room, they survived a shoot-out with such realistic sound effects they had to check themselves for bullet holes. Someone in their group yelled, "I'm hit!" which brought nervous laughter and more screaming.

The final scene was a shockingly realistic cemetery at night with quivering tombstones and zombies popping up from behind them. Alice wanted to close her eyes and think of something happy like wedding cake with elegant fondant and buttercream icing. Wedding gowns with layers and layers of tulle with sequined lace. Bridesmaids who all matched and cooperated happily with the bride no matter what their personal opinions were. Groomsmen who didn't wear their rented tuxedos as if they were straitjackets.

Yes, those were her happy thoughts.

Despite the utter terror of the experience, Alice tried to cling to two rational thoughts. The company Starlight Point had hired to frighten its guests nearly to an early grave was worth every penny. And, despite being startled into screaming more often than she cared to admit, she wasn't truly afraid because a warm, strong hand gripped hers the entire time. A familiar hand that brought with it years of feelings she'd believed hidden.

When her group spilled through the back door, Haley nearly collapsed on the ground, breathing heavily and fanning herself. "Want to do it again?" she asked.

"Are you nuts? I thought you were going

to faint in there," Alice said. "You were terrified."

"That's part of the fun. It's the same feeling at the top of a roller coaster hill just before you go over. The good kind of terror," Haley said.

Alice tried to slow her racing heart. "I think I've just discovered our target demographic. Eighteen-year-olds with healthy hearts and a sadistic side."

Nate laughed quietly next to her and she turned, realizing he was still gripping her hand. As soon as they made eye contact, he released her hand and took one step back. *I guess the battlefield bonding is over*, she thought. Despite the quick distance Nate put between them, Haley must have noticed the hand-holding, however justified it was by the terrifying experience in the haunted house. She just hoped Haley wouldn't say anything.

"I'm done for the night," Nate announced. He lingered for a moment, shifting his weight from one foot to the other, and then he turned and walked into the deepening dusk.

"What happened to him?" Haley asked. "Too scared, you think?"

"I don't know," Alice said, even though the

truth wanted to fight its way from her chest. Something had happened, but she didn't know what to call it.

TAKING ADVANTAGE OF THE MIDWEEK QUIET, Alice walked an engaged couple through the haunted house with the lights on and no actors or sound effects. Their wedding was actually taking place on the haunted trail amid the spooky decorations on Halloween night, but they wanted to see the haunted house just for fun. It was an odd request, but Alice wanted to keep her customers happy. As it turned out, the trip through the haunted house was the least frightening part of her meeting with the couple.

Kayleen and Keith. Their names sounded almost cute together, but after spending two hours with them, Alice felt certain their marriage would last an agonizing and tempest-filled two years at the most.

They fought about the date, which had already been booked for months. Keith had apparently told his family the wrong date and Kayleen had gloated about being in the right, even though it was only a matter of one day—October 30 versus October 31. *Strike one*.

They fought about which horror flick had the best gruesome special effects, even though it was completely off topic. Alice was astonished to learn so many slasher movies had actually been made. *Strike two*.

Strike three came as Alice asked them to select menu items for the reception, which would be held under the big tent in the Wonderful West. To her amazement, the lovebirds fought over potato salad's merits as compared to cole slaw. Bride and groom both invoked the nuclear option of attacking each other's families, comparing each other's mothers in drastically unflattering ways.

"Perhaps your guests will enjoy the reception either way," Alice suggested. "We could come back to that decision after we've worked out the details on the music and decorations."

Her tone was appropriate and patient because this was not her first wedding where the bride and groom (or their families) quibbled over details that were drops in a bucket compared to long years of marriage and its compromises.

Despite her outward appearance of professional courtesy and interest, Alice was more uneasy than she had ever been while planning a wedding. This was her twentieth wedding at Starlight Point. It ought to be some kind of milestone. Instead, all she could imagine was what married life would be like for Kayleen and Keith.

She should tell them the truth, that she believed they shouldn't get married anytime soon. They'd be angry, and Starlight Point would lose their business, but wasn't the truth worth sacrificing for, no matter how much it might hurt?

While they battled over the color of balloons—black or orange or both—Alice walked over to Virginia and Henry, who were replacing damaged pumpkins in one of the displays in front of the antique cars.

"Squirrels strike again," Henry said. "Their lack of manners is staggering. They can't eat the easy to reach pumpkins and squash on the outside row. They go right for the middle every time just so I have to tiptoe in."

"And face near death when I throw him replacements," Virginia said as she lined up a shot and tossed a small pumpkin to her partner.

Alice sat on the railing surrounding the fall garden. "I might want to trade you anyway. Those two," she said, nodding toward the prospective bride and groom, who were across the midway, hands-on-hips arguing under the tent, "are getting married on Halloween eve."

"Scary," Virginia said.

"You don't know the half of it. So far, they've fought over every detail. He even said her mother should come dressed as a vampire because she would suck the fun right out of the wedding."

Henry laughed.

"It's not funny," Alice said. "Someone should go over there and tell them they're not ready to get married if they honestly plan to have wedding rings shaped like skulls and she thinks his newest tattoo looks too much like his ex-girlfriend."

Virginia and Henry exchanged a glance.

"I'm not making that up," Alice said.

"That's what we were afraid of. So," Virginia asked as she leaned on the railing next to Alice, "why don't you march over there and tell them either they shouldn't get married or they deserve each other?"

"I'm afraid it wouldn't help."

"You mean they'd do it anyway?" Henry asked.

Alice shook her head. "I think they need a therapist who appreciates their sense of humor and their…"

"Good taste and judgment?" Virginia asked. "Good luck with that."

"They have almost three weeks until the big day," Alice said.

Henry nodded. "Plenty of time to get that tattoo altered and special order those unique rings."

"You can't help some people," Virginia said. "You just have to let them make their own mistakes. And not too many people are brave enough to call off a wedding right before it happens."

Alice sighed.

"Cheer up," Henry said. "Perhaps they're getting all their fighting out of the way before they get married and live happily ever after."

"I better get back over there and see if they're willing to take my advice against having black icing on their cake," Alice said.

"Unless you want your guests to have black tongues, it's not the best choice."

Wedding number twenty on Halloween night was going to be her scariest one yet.

CHAPTER ELEVEN

PARENTS, GRANDPARENTS and kids wearing Halloween costumes streamed through the front gates for the first ever Starlight Point Community Halloween Party.

To open the party, Jack Hamilton addressed the crowd. "We're both a trick and a treat," he said, smiling and charming the large group gathered at the front gates. "And we want to say thank you for helping Starlight Point have another great year."

Dozens of employees had volunteered to work the afternoon event, and the vendors had opened their stands. Instead of selling hot dogs and fries, though, they were handing out candy in the spirit of the holiday, which was still a couple weeks away.

Alice almost wished she'd worn a costume. She'd loved dressing up when she was a child. Even more than free Halloween candy, she'd loved making a costume with her grandmother. She vividly remembered having coordinated princess gowns with her two sisters in pink, green and blue. She had chosen pink. Both of her sisters lived in different states now, but Alice treasured the picture her dad had taken of the three of them in their princess gowns on the front steps of their house.

She still lived in that house where her unworn wedding gown hung in the spare bedroom's closet. Maybe it was time for a change.

"I'm here as a grandma tonight," Virginia told Alice as they walked down the main midway to the first food and activity station.

"I can tell," Alice said, laughing.

Virginia wore a fairy godmother costume complete with wings and a sparkling tiara. "June fixed me up with this costume," she explained, "which you could probably already guess from how sparkly it is."

"I thought so," Alice said. "And I'm insanely jealous."

Waving her magic wand, Virginia was surrounded by grandchildren. The oldest, Ross, was nine but still young enough to wear an astronaut costume. He held his little sister's hand. At almost two, Abigail toddled precariously along the concrete in her princess costume. Her tiara had slid sideways and the purple netting under her skirt stuck out, but she was adorable. Augusta and Jack's little girl, Nora, held her grandmother's hand. She was dressed as a cowgirl and wore a big hat she could barely see out from underneath.

Each of Virginia's grandchildren clutched an orange bucket with the Starlight Point logo on the side. The candy pails were free for local children, and all they had to do was fill it with candy at the food and ride stands along the midway. For parents, it was a fun and safe event, and they could also enjoy a complimentary cup of hot cider and a dough-nut or apple fritter.

One of her granddaughters tugged on her hand, and Virginia smiled apologetically at Alice. "Sorry I can't help out tonight, but I'm the babysitter since my kids are all hosting the party."

"I think you're having more fun this way," Alice said.

"I know I am."

Alice joined the volunteers handing out suckers from the table in front of the cable cars platform. The air smelled like fall eve-nings from when she was young. She remembered raking leaves and having a small fire in their backyard with her friends. Nate had come over and they'd sat watching the fire until the stars were bright.

Alice imagined her nieces in costumes and regretted she hadn't called her sisters to see if a road trip for Halloween was possible. Holidays were more fun with children. At twenty-seven, Alice was beginning to wonder if she'd be the last of the Birmingham sisters to get married. Five years ago, she was in line to be the first.

Out of the darkness, Nate appeared and snapped a picture of a little boy dropping candy into his orange container. He talked with the boy's mother and wrote something on a notebook he drew from his jacket pocket. When he saw Alice, he walked over to her. "I missed fall nights like this when I lived in Florida."

"No flannel weather there?" Alice asked, surprised Nate was starting a conversation with a semi-personal comment.

"Only once or twice during the winter. And flannel was probably overkill even at that." He drew a deep breath and looked up at the sky. "I like the smell of leaves and the cool air."

Was that why he chose the damp forest smell for his soap or cologne? Did it remind him of home?

"I was just thinking about that," Alice said. "How much I like autumn."

He leaned on the staircase leading to the platform of the cable cars. Night insects swirled around him as he took a few more pictures. His camera flash lit up kids in colorful costumes from a distance. A little girl in a bunny costume stopped for candy, and a boy wearing a green dinosaur creation bumped into her. They both laughed and held out their orange buckets.

"My favorite costume as a kid was a sheriff's outfit," Nate said. "I had a real badge I borrowed from my uncle, but he wouldn't let me use his gun. I pretended my orange plastic one was real anyway. I think I shot every tree, mailbox and squirrel in the neighborhood that night."

"Does your uncle still live in Bayside?"

Nate nodded. "But he's retired now and spends the winter in Florida. He's leaving next week."

Alice handed out candy and complimented children on their costumes. She wanted to ask about Nate's father and whether his doctors thought he would make it through a long cold Michigan winter, but she was afraid to throw an obstacle in the middle of the conversation—a friendly and unfettered one for once.

"My sisters and I had matching princess costumes one year," she said, "but I was pretty fond of my mermaid costume. I had to take really tiny steps because of the tail."

"That's the fun part," Nate said. "Taking risks for free candy. Is this more fun than organizing weddings?" he asked.

"Less complicated," Alice admitted. "It involves pageantry and planning, but children know exactly what they want and their demands are simple. And there aren't usually disagreements and sticky situations unless somebody doesn't want to trade candy."

The tiny steps she'd taken in that mermaid outfit seemed like huge leaps compared to the mincing steps she and Nate were taking toward the one thing they didn't want to talk about. Alice took a breath and resolved to take a chance on honesty. They were adults. College graduates. Not uncertain youths driven by hormones, emotions and public opinion. What if she came out and asked him if he would be willing to talk about where they had gone wrong?

Unless he had changed drastically, he'd run away dodging pumpkins and candy buckets.

"Speaking of difficult situations, I heard about the Halloween couple with the skull rings and tattoos," Nate said.

Back to small talk, when what they really needed was something life-sized.

Alice leaned over the table and handed a girl a pink sucker. "I love your superhero costume," she told the girl. Alice turned her attention back to Nate. "I'm surprised you heard about the wedding couple from the dark side."

"Henry told me you were wrangling some tough customers in the Wonderful West."

She shrugged and handed out three more suckers. "The good news is they fought with each other instead of turning on me. I thought that was a temporary win."

"Tell me their wedding does not involve the train."

Alice laughed and looked up. Nate was smiling broadly and his eyes wrinkled at the corners. This surface conversation was nice and Alice wanted to enjoy it, but she was fooling herself. She and Nate weren't friends, and she was kidding herself by pretending they could be.

If Alice was interested in putting on a happy face and living a lie, she would have married Nate five years ago.

"No, it doesn't involve the train. And if I had my way, I'd force them to postpone their wedding until they can agree on balloons and frosting. I'd say their marriage doesn't stand a chance and they should call it off."

Nate physically flinched and took one step backward. "It wouldn't be good for you professionally to encourage the loss of business and revenue for Starlight Point."

His tone sent ripples of anger through Alice, and she knew the small talk was over. "As you found out the hard way, I'll decide what's good for me even if someone else doesn't like it."

"MIND IF I join you?" Henry asked as he strode alongside Virginia. He hadn't planned to impose upon her family time, but he couldn't resist. Virginia's long blue-and-silver gown sparkled in the lights and he wanted to be close enough to see if the blue matched her eyes. "I noticed you have your hands full."

"In the best way," she said, smiling at her grandkids. "But you can come along with us in case somebody gets tired of walking."

"They look like they're going strong, but I'd love to team up with you. I look silly at this event by myself."

Henry opened his hands as an offer to pick up either Nora or Abigail, but they both shook their heads and shrank back toward their grandmother.

"It's a shy age," Virginia said. "Nothing personal. They've never seen you before."

Henry had seen them from a distance but always in a crowd. They probably didn't view him as a friend of their grandmother, and the thought made him feel oddly left out.

"Good thing I didn't wear the costume I planned," he said. "It might have scared them."

Virginia laughed and Ross looked interested. "What was your costume gonna be?" Ross asked.

"Airline pilot. Wings and all."

"Cool," Ross said. "But not scary, even to girls. Is it a real pilot's uniform?"

"Yes. I used to wear it almost every day."

"Why didn't you wear it tonight?"

Henry smiled. "Believe it or not, I was afraid I was too old and people would laugh at me."

"Grandma wore a costume," Ross said. "And no one laughed at her."

"You've got me there. I guess your grandmother is much braver than I am, and she has a much better costume."

"Who says it's a costume?" Virginia asked. "Maybe I am a fairy godmother."

Ross laughed, took both girls by the hand and walked up to the candy station at the loading platform of the Silver Streak, leaving Virginia and Henry alone but watching from close by.

"I thought you might be working tonight," Virginia said. "Or volunteering is more like it."

"I did for a while. I helped set up and hauled big bags of candy to all the stations, but they don't need me right now. I'll stick around and clean up, though."

"It'll be a late night for you."

"Not that late," Henry said, inching closer to Virginia. "After you finish grandma duty, how about having a glass of wine with me downtown? I keep hearing about a nice wine bar down by the water, but it doesn't seem right to go in there by myself."

Virginia glanced at her grandchildren, who were slowly making their way back from the candy line. "I don't know. It may be a while before I could get away."

"I'll wait. The park's not open tomorrow, so we could live it up and stay out as late as we want," Henry said.

"Maybe I could call you."

Henry was about to agree and consider the concession a victory, but loud screaming stopped him. He and Virginia snapped their heads to the source of the crying and Virginia started running toward her granddaughter who'd gotten tangled in her dress and fallen on the concrete midway. They rushed to her side and Virginia picked her up and held her close.

"It's okay, baby," she said. "Did you scrape your knee?"

"I tried to hold on to her hand," Ross said. "But she started running to get back to you."

Henry felt helpless and guilty. Virginia had been distracted talking to him. He was trying to set up a date, thinking only of spending more time with her.

"Don't worry, Ross, little kids surprise you all the time," Virginia said. "Your stepmother was one of the worst, always dancing away from me when I least expected it."

June raced up out of nowhere and took her daughter from her mother. The little girl started crying all over again as Ross explained what happened.

"Sorry, June," Virginia said. "I took my eyes off her for one second."

June laughed. "It's the dress. She hasn't yet mastered the art of being graceful in a costume. That'll come with time." June held her daughter on one hip and carried her candy bucket in the other hand. "I'll take her on a round of candy stops for a few minutes and then I'll bring her back. She'll forget all about it. Want me to take the other kids, too?"

June flicked a glance between Henry and Virginia as she asked.

"Not at all," Virginia said quickly.

Henry felt as if he was a burglar lurking and listening to a family dinner while hiding in the broom closet. He'd distracted Virginia and put her in a sticky situation. Little kids fell down all the time, he didn't need to be a dad or a grandfather to know that. But Virginia had stiffened toward him in the last two minutes. Did she feel guilty because she was talking to him instead of watching the kids?

He wanted to renew his offer of a late night wine date, but he felt selfish and awkward bringing it up.

"See you tomorrow," Virginia said as she gave him a quick smile and walked away, holding hands with her two grandchildren.

He turned and headed for a small shed where extra trash cans were stored. It was never too early to start cleaning up the mess from the party.

CHAPTER TWELVE

"I ALMOST WISH the Hamiltons had said no when I asked permission to close part of the Western Trail for this wedding," Alice told Haley. "I made a big effort to sell the idea as something special and once-in-a-lifetime, and it was one of the first weddings we booked."

"Maybe it'll be fine. Everyone's in the holiday spirit."

"If it goes badly, there will be far too many witnesses—the park will be open during the ceremony."

"What are you worried about?" Haley asked. "You've done all the preparation you usually do. Every single detail is planned."

"Everything we can predict is planned. And while the unpredictable things can be the fun part—usually—about weddings, they can also be the nightmares you see on social media."

"Spooky wedding goes to the devil," Haley said, making big air quotes with her fingers.

"No," Alice moaned. "I should have listened to my gut instincts about this couple and told them to get married in a graveyard somewhere or, better yet, not get married at all."

Haley narrowed her eyes. "If they aren't right for each other, how did they get this far? They're pledging a lifetime of commitment in only a matter of hours."

Alice felt a familiar stab of regret. "I think they got caught up in the event itself. Halloween is one of the areas where they connect, with their shared love of the maudlin and grotesque. What if the ceremony and the fun of planning it is half their motivation for getting married in the first place? Then they're really in trouble."

Haley shook her head. "I can't imagine anyone getting so swept along in party planning that they'd marry someone they didn't really want to marry in the first place."

Alice sighed. "It happens. Believe me. Some brides want the fairy tale and if they sample enough cake and try on enough dresses, it will make Mr. Wrong turn into Mr. Right."

"That's the most cynical thing I've ever heard you say. You're brutally honest," Haley said, "but this is crazy talk coming from the woman who organizes those tastings and fittings."

Alice considered telling Haley her big secret, but there was already too much drama in the air. Haley would ask for details, and that would be a dangerous foray into things she was better off not bringing up right before a major Starlight Point event. And if Haley asked questions about the groom himself... what would she say?

Nate was affable and well-liked. Telling his coworkers he had been emotionally distant, kept his feelings under guard and she hadn't been sure he loved her would not go over well. Especially if she said the truly nuclear thing—that she had loved him too much to marry him if she couldn't be assured of having his entire heart.

People would not understand.

"We should check on Mr. and Mrs. Halloween Wedding," Alice said.

"Sure," Haley agreed. "Now that you've ruined any romantic ideas I ever had about weddings."

"Not ruined. Just tempered by reality. Our current reality involves getting the ceremony done on time and this part of the park reopened as soon as possible."

The Western Trail could only be closed temporarily on a busy Saturday night, so the reception would be held in the ballroom, which was closed to guests most of the time anyway. Alice had pictured a wonderful procession of the wedding party and all the wedding guests, dressed in elaborate costumes, parading up the midway to the ballroom. It would be a free Halloween parade for Starlight Point guests.

If it went well.

At each end of the Western Trail, guests showed their invitations and made it past security. Since this was the first wedding happening while the park was open, Starlight Point had negotiated group discount rates for anyone attending the wedding.

The bride and groom had the use of two back rooms in side-by-side, old-fashioned gift shops in order to dress and prepare. At Alice's signal, they would join the rest of the wedding party under a giant arch draped with black bunting, skeletons and sinister decorations.

"How's it going in there?" Alice called through the door of the dressing area the bride was using.

She heard a hiccup in return.

"Need any help with your dress?"

This time the answer was a long belch.

"I'm coming in," Alice called cheerfully. She pushed through the door and found the bride and her sister sitting on the floor in their underclothes. "The wedding starts in ten minutes," she said. "Let me help you into your dresses." Alice leaned back out the door. "Haley," she called. "Can you come in here?"

Alice took a bottle of bourbon from the bride and set it up high on a shelf.

"Are they all out there?" the bride asked.

Alice nodded. "Your guests are lined up and waiting along the Western Trail. Almost all of them wore costumes, just as you asked."

"Humph," said Kayleen, the bride. She hoisted herself to her feet. "I don't think I look good in my dress. I gained some weight after I ordered it last spring."

Alice had noticed. She'd tried to find a tactful way to get the bride to come to the bridal shop downtown for a fitting check. She'd said it was her policy to always go with brides for the final check, just in case of a faulty zipper or uneven hemline. It was a minor fib, but it was in the interest of tact and making sure the bride felt comfortable on her special day.

But Kayleen had refused to go to the dressmaker and assured Alice the dress was fine.

"Let's see," Alice said.

Haley was helping the bride's sister into a dark purple dress that shimmered and sagged precariously while she zipped it up the back. Haley gave Alice a look that said *good luck*.

She removed the wedding dress from its plastic bag and barely restrained her gasp when she saw it. *It was black*. Shimmering with sequins and cheap glitter. Spaghetti straps. And, judging with her experienced eye, Alice was certain it was a good two sizes too small. *At least the fabric is interwoven with elastic*. Sadly, the black stretchy material would have been more appropriate for a bathing suit.

"Pretty, ain't it?"

Alice smiled and nodded, hating herself for lying. "Stunning. Your guests will never forget this day, and neither will you."

"Ya think?" The bride fingered the fabric.

"I wanted just these little straps so my tattoos would show."

"Of course," Alice said, "that's part of who you are." Despite her encouraging all-for-one and one-for-all tone, Alice wondered what the tattoos looked like. Something from a horror flick?

"I've got a black crow to put on my shoulder, too."

Haley glanced up and Alice was afraid to make eye contact with her. *Is this for real?*

"Is it alive?" Genuine alarm threatened to creep into Alice's voice. She really wished she had been more of a dictator on the details of this wedding. She always got involved in flowers, food, decorations, logistics, invitations, et cetera. But the actual wedding gown and the hair and makeup choices were something she left to the bride and her mother, sisters or friends. Unless asked, Alice didn't comment on the style of gowns or the cut of men's tuxedos.

From now on, she was going to ask more questions.

"It's a fake bird. It pins to my shoulder strap and talks if you pull the cord."

"What a fun novelty," Alice said.

A loud pounding on the door startled them.

"Can you come out here and tie this lousy necktie?" Alice recognized the groom's voice.

"We're not decent," the bride said.

"So? I've already seen everything you've got," Keith replied.

"You're a jerk," Kayleen yelled through the door. "Go away so you don't see me before the wedding."

"Told you I've already seen it all," the man muttered. "Who's gonna tie this thing?"

Alice went to the door and opened it a crack. "Can't your groomsmen help you?"

He laughed bitterly. "They can't tie a tie sober. And they ain't sober."

"I'll call someone. Go back to your dressing room and wait there."

"Who are you calling?" Haley asked.

"Nate. I know he's out there with his camera, and I know for certain he can handle a necktie."

Alice dialed Nate and was relieved when he picked up. They had not spoken a word since the community Halloween party, but she needed him now. She made her request, and he didn't hesitate, assuring her he was right outside already taking pictures of the wedding location. His voice was smooth in the *everything's fine* PR manner he wore like a shield.

"I don't care if he gets that thing tied," Kayleen said. "I don't even think Keith wants to marry me."

"Of course he does. Arms up," Alice said as she held up the glittering black dress and tried to coax it down Kayleen's body. Kayleen smelled of sweat and alcohol, and Alice held her breath and wondered if she'd made the right career choice. She also wondered if there was any chance of the zipper closing and surviving the day's events.

"You look great," Haley told the bride's sister. She wore a purple dress with spiderwebs made of rows of glitter and sequins. Like the bride, the maid of honor had long artificially black hair that stood out almost grotesquely against her fair skin.

"Beautiful," Alice concurred. "Haley, can you help me with this zipper?"

With Haley holding both sides of the dress within an inch of each other and Alice operating the zipper, they squeezed the bride into the black gown. Alice wondered how Nate was doing with the groom and pictured him patiently tying the man's tie and straightening his collar. It was nice to be able to call him and ask the favor. The only other person she could think of was Henry, and she had him supervising the crowd waiting for the ceremony to start.

There was a knock at the door. "Alice," someone whispered urgently. *Was that Nate's voice?*

"I'll get the bird wired up if you need to go," Haley said.

"I need my veil," Kayleen complained. "It wasn't in the bag with my dress."

Alice took a deep breath and answered the door.

"Can you come out here?" Nate asked.

"I must have left my veil at home," Kayleen said as Alice left the room. Great, that was a problem she could only solve with time. And they didn't have any time. The wedding was supposed to start in five minutes. Maybe four.

Alice closed the door behind her and followed Nate a few steps away from the back of the gift shop. A disc jockey played spooky Halloween tunes to entertain the wedding crowd just a dozen yards away. Some of them were dancing instead of waiting patiently for the ceremony to begin. With their costumes, the assembled guests had the appearance of being at a Halloween party instead of a wedding.

"Couldn't you get the groom into his tie?" Alice asked. She and Nate stood so close together she could smell the comforting damp forest smell he exuded. She'd rather be hiking through a forest with him right now. They used to go for long walks in the woods where they could be alone, talk and kiss.

"The tie is the least of his problems."

"What do you mean? What happened?"

"Cold feet. Very, very cold. Ice cold. Arctic cold. Frozen section at the supermarket cold—"

"I get it," Alice said. "When you say cold feet, do you mean he's very, very nervous, or do you think he's actually planning to not go through with the ceremony?"

"The second one, I think."

Alice crossed her arms. "How many weddings have you helped with?"

Nate wrinkled his brow and Alice sincerely hoped he was not going to mention the one she'd almost had with him.

"Not that many. My sister's." He hesitated a moment. "And the train one here. You remember how that one went. I've been to lots of them, but I wasn't backstage crew."

"So…it's possible that the groom's just blowing off steam. Nervous, but not seriously thinking of backing out with a crowd of two hundred people dancing around in costumes right behind my back."

Alice had purposely turned her back to the partiers so she could only see Nate and concentrate on the problem at hand.

"Hard to say. He said some pretty damning things about the bride's family."

"That happens."

"And the bride's…associations with some of the other members of the wedding party," Nate added.

"Okay," Alice said. She bit her lip. "That also happens. Sometimes."

"And her habit of drinking right out of bourbon bottles in mixed company."

Alice took a deep breath. Her last five minutes with Kayleen had certainly not made Alice want to spend the rest of her life with the woman, but certainly there had to be redeeming qualities that had brought Kayleen and Keith together in the first place.

"Maybe I should talk to him, remind him of all the things he loves about her and reassure him that his feelings of nervousness right now are completely natural," Alice said.

Nate raised one eyebrow.

Please don't take this moment to remind me I walked out on you right before our wedding. My nerves can't take it.

He said nothing.

Thank you.

She had to fix this. If the wedding fell apart, the assembled guests would go home. The Hamiltons would regret agreeing to Alice's risky request to close the Western Trail. The cake and food in the ballroom would go to waste. Every wedding guest would remember this wedding not for its uniqueness but instead for its failure.

Alice's cheeks were burning with the friction of her decision. Her conscience and belief that the wedding shouldn't happen—at least not today—were battling with her love for her work at Starlight Point.

"Here he comes," Nate said. He nodded at someone behind Alice. "I hope you can work some magic or we're all going to look like fools," he whispered.

Alice spun around. "Keith," she said. "This is the most important day of your life, so you're allowed to break the rules just a little bit. Why don't you come with me to see the bride for a few minutes before the wedding?"

Keith scratched his neck where his black shirt collar met his untied necktie. "I don't know if that's a good idea."

"Trust me," Alice said. "I'm a professional wedding planner."

Keith crossed his arms over his chest. He wore a black suit and black shirt. Instead of a lapel pin, he had a skull shaped from rhinestones pinned to his jacket. "Well then, maybe you can magically change my bride into someone I want to be chained to till divorce do us part."

"Come with me," she said. She took his arm and led him toward the door separating him from Kayleen. Alice just hoped Haley had done something about the bride's makeup, kept the bourbon on the top shelf and attached the talking bird in an attractive way.

This could still work out.

As she approached the door and knocked, Alice was glad Nate was right behind her.

The bride herself whipped open the door and swayed a little with the movement. She had a black spiderweb down one side of her face. Alice was amazed at the quick makeup work while she'd been outside, but then she realized it was a temporary tattoo. With dark red lipstick and a black bird on her shoulder, Kayleen looked like a horror movie bride. Alice had to admit that although it wasn't traditional, the bride was true to herself, making her wedding her own.

Kayleen burped and wiped her mouth with the back of her hand.

Alice heard Nate sigh behind her. She took a deep breath, grabbed the groom's arm and pulled him into the dressing room.

"YOU CAN'T BE SERIOUS," Nate said as he stood with Alice behind the temporary dressing room. "You talked them out of it?"

His frustration vibrated from him and his voice was far too loud, but he couldn't help it.

"I didn't talk them out of it," Alice said. She crossed her arms over her chest. The red flush creeping up her neck almost matched her auburn hair. "I just didn't talk them into doing something they might regret the rest of their lives."

"Going through with the wedding is something they would regret the rest of their lives?" Nate said. "That's your opinion, as I found out the hard way."

"Whoa," June said as she and Evie slipped around the side of the building. "I thought Keith and Kayleen were the feuding couple, not you two."

Nate clenched his teeth together and felt his jaw muscle popping. This was not his professional persona.

Alice blew out a breath and her shoulders lowered. "We're not a feuding couple."

"Then what did you mean when you said—?"

Evie elbowed June and a heavy silence hung over them despite the distant sounds of roller coasters and music. Nate wanted to ask June exactly what she'd heard, but he concentrated instead on maintaining a neutral expression. The wedding failure was not, technically, his fault or his responsibility. If Alice wanted to sink herself by sticking to some moral code of brutal honesty, it wasn't his problem.

But it was a good reminder that he should watch his words and moves around her.

"Haley called," Evie said. "She told us the wedding might not happen and asked us to come out and do damage control. How much damage do we have?"

"And is the wedding happening?" June added.

Alice shook her head. She didn't look disappointed or upset. Did she seem vindicated, even pleased? How could she?

"You couldn't talk them into going through with it?" June asked.

"I didn't," Alice said. "At first I tried, but then I backed off. People shouldn't get married unless they're absolutely sure."

"This was one of the things I worried about when we decided to add the wedding packages," Evie said. "Nothing says drama like a wedding, and Starlight Point doesn't usually need any extra drama."

"So now what?" Nate interjected. "Are you going to tell the guests to just go about their business, maybe hit a haunted house on the way out, forget the whole thing?"

"This is bad," Evie groaned. "I hate seeing

guests disappointed. What if this is their first
and only visit to Starlight Point?"

Alice focused on the ground but Nate could
still see her expression. Any satisfaction he
might have seen a moment ago had disappeared. Did she fear getting fired, or at least
losing the Hamiltons' good opinion?

Whether Alice deserved a way out or not,
Starlight Point did. He was the public relations
man, and this was his opportunity to prove his
worth and do what he did best—assure everyone that everything was just fine.

"Maybe it's not a disaster," Nate said.
All three women focused on him, listening.
"What if we turn the wedding reception into
a Halloween party for the guests who are here
anyway? If I can get Kayleen and Keith to act
as host and hostess at a party without getting
married or calling it a reception, their guests
will still parade to the ballroom and eat that
beautiful wedding cake with the black frosting. Other guests at Starlight Point won't be
the wiser, and the party preparations won't
go to waste. We save face."

Alice flashed him a smile. "That's an
amazing idea. I'll go talk to Kayleen and

Keith and see if I can get them to agree to this."

"No," Nate said.

Alice's smile faded and her cheeks paled.

"I think you've done enough talking," Nate said neutrally. A bystander might have thought he was trying to spare her any extra labor or effort, but he and Alice both knew the truth. "I'll smooth this one over."

"Whew," Evie said. "You're a lifesaver, Nate."

Evie and June walked away smiling, but Alice shot him a look that suggested she wouldn't accept a life ring from him even if she was treading water in choppy waves.

CHAPTER THIRTEEN

NATE LEANED AGAINST the closed door of his father's hospital room and stared at the yellowed floor. They were in the older section of the Bayside Hospital, and his father was sleeping under the watchful eyes of the nurses and the slow drip of the IV antibiotics. When Nate had arrived home on Halloween night after a busy and tumultuous failed wedding, he'd found his father huddled in front of the fireplace. He'd bundled him into the car and driven straight to the hospital despite his dad's feeble protests.

"I'm glad you called me," Nate's uncle Warren said as he put an arm around Nate's shoulders. "I can't believe how fast Murray went downhill."

"Not downhill. Just a close call. When he went in for his chemo treatment, they told us any infection could be bad. He already had a fever over a hundred when I got home last night."

Nate had had no doubt his father needed to go to the hospital, and he was thankful his quick call to his dad's oncologist helped them bypass the emergency room. His memories of walking through those doors fifteen years earlier still sliced him raw. He couldn't walk back out of the hospital without his father.

"How long do you think they'll keep him?" his uncle asked.

"At least a day, maybe more, depending on how he responds to the antibiotics."

His uncle nodded. "We're leaving for Florida in another week, but we'll stick around if you need us. My wife wouldn't mind spending Thanksgiving at home."

"We'll be okay. Dad and I have been through a lot."

"You have. Never saw anyone braver than Murray, not even among my fellow police officers. He was really strong for you and your sister after...what happened."

Nate wondered if Warren knew his brother had cried at night in his bedroom when he thought no one could hear him. Nate had stood outside his father's closed door many times in his early teens, wondering if he should go in. Fear had stopped him every time. Fear that he would break down and be the one consoled instead of consoling. He'd broken down at his mother's funeral, and the image the photographer from the local paper had captured still haunted him. His tearstained and devastated face had been the centerpiece of the newspaper's anti-drunk driving campaign for a year after his mother's death. As a police officer, his uncle had led the charge and received accolades for his work, but Nate had been ashamed every time that picture ran in the paper.

"Always admired how tough you all were," Uncle Warren continued. "It's the only way to face things."

If Alice were here, she'd have something to say about that.

Nate's spontaneous thought shocked him. Why was he thinking about her at one in the morning? Her particular brand of honesty would throw a major wrinkle in the perfectly smooth relationship he had with his uncle. Keep it light, avoid emotional displays, offer manly support up to a certain point. Maintain the appearance that everything's fine.

Alice would ask Uncle Warren what he was hiding under that flimsy veneer and why he wasn't giving his nephew a hug right now instead of standing shoulder to shoulder as if they were facing an enemy battalion.

"Do you need anything?" his uncle asked. "Coffee? A ride home? Change for the vending machine in the lounge?"

"I'm not a teenager," Nate said, smiling. "I have cash and a car. I'll probably go home soon because there's nothing I can do here. I'll check in with work and come back later in the morning."

"Keep me posted," his uncle said. He patted him on the shoulder and strode away with a straight spine, as if he'd just issued sensible orders on how to face the fact that Nate's father was slowly dying.

Nate turned and looked through the window to his father's room. His eyes blurred with tears and he was glad the nurse had her back turned so there was no one to see him *almost* cry.

SNOWFALL DURING THE first week of November wasn't unusual in Michigan, but Virginia marveled at how different Starlight Point looked when it was open for business while covered with snow. Seeing lights and holiday decorations through the drifting snowflakes made her family amusement park look like a strange and new land.

Gladys danced happily at the end of her leash and pulled it from Virginia's grip. Henry grabbed for the leash, but Virginia laughed. "Let her go. She can't get in too much trouble, and I can always lure her back with the treats in my pocket."

"I feel as if I'm getting away with something. I'm in an empty amusement park in the snow with a beautiful woman."

Virginia sucked in the cold, wintry air. "The park is not officially closed, just on weeknights like this." She shuddered and Henry put an arm around her.

"I could give you my coat," he offered.

"Then you'd be cold, too. If we keep walking we'll warm up. Especially if we have to chase Gladys." As she and Henry passed the quiet carousel and the closed food stands on the midway, their footsteps were muffled by the snow. But Virginia could still hear the sounds of Starlight Point that were written on her heart. How many times had she strolled the midways with Ford? Every patch of concrete under the snow and the vacant cable cars overhead still sung with his memory.

Henry caught her hand and strode alongside her, swinging her arm cheerfully. They both wore gloves, but she still felt the warmth of his fingers. "It was a great Halloween last weekend with the kids and costumes," he said.

"The wedding was a disaster, but the rest of the weekend was perfect, including the weather. I'm glad the snow waited a few days."

"I'm ready to fast forward through Thanksgiving and get right to Christmas," Henry said. "And the festivities we're having here."

"Don't rush," Virginia said. *Life goes much too fast.* For a time after Ford died, her entire world had slowed down, but lately it had seemed to swirl faster like the snowflakes around them. Her family was growing, the Point expanding its season, and she wasn't alone in the snow.

Gladys ran ahead and jumped up on the bench where the path split and led to the Wonderful West.

Ford's bench. A place he'd loved to sit and

watch the crowds advance down the midway. And it was where he'd lain down to die alone on a spring morning before the park opened more than five years ago.

"I think your dog must have found something interesting on that bench," Henry commented.

Virginia's heart was colder than the steel structures of the roller coasters. She wanted to call Gladys back, lure her in with treats instead of approaching her as Gladys licked the bench furiously.

Ford's bench. Tears stung her eyes and contrasted sharply with the cold air. What if Ford were there now, watching over her and all of Starlight Point? Would he want her to move on? What would he think of Henry, the tall man swinging her arm and urging her toward the bench she always avoided.

Evie loved that bench and often sat there just to feel close to her father, but Virginia had never been that brave. She always hoped someone was already sitting on it when she went by.

What was on it now?

Henry reached the bench a few steps before Virginia and grabbed hold of Gladys's

202 BACK TO THE LAKE BREEZE HOTEL

collar. He laughed and the sound echoed off the nearby roller coasters.

"Leftover Halloween candy," he said. "Suckers and licorice. Glad it's not chocolate or we'd have a serious problem."

Gladys looked at Virginia with happy eyes, her tongue slapping the edges of her mouth and lapping up the sugary treat left by a child from the Halloween weekend.

"You're sweet enough already, Gladys," Virginia said. "You should…you should let that go."

Henry put an arm around Virginia and pulled her close. His lips brushed her forehead at the edge of her knitted cap. His mouth moved lower and a kiss trailed along her cheek. Virginia closed her eyes, imagining how nice it would be to let herself be drawn in by his warmth and tenderness. She'd missed that in the years she'd built her own life since Ford's passing.

Building her own life so she could never again be completely devastated by the loss of another person had been her goal and lifesaving mission for five years of holidays. Five Thanksgivings, Christmases and first snowfalls.

It was too soon to give up on the thing that had pulled her through the darkest times.

"It's getting colder," Virginia said. "Time to go home."

THE NEXT MORNING, Virginia met Alice in her office to go over upcoming special events.

"Henry is bringing coffee," Alice said. "We need it with this cold weather. I'm certainly thankful to use this time for indoor planning instead of being out there with the crews taking down and putting away the Halloween decorations."

"Look who I found at the coffeepot," Henry announced as he came through Alice's door with Nate behind him. Nate lingered in the doorframe.

"How is your father?" Virginia asked. "I heard he was in the hospital the past few days."

Nate smiled, but Virginia noticed lines of fatigue around his eyes and mouth. "Better now. It was an infection, but it's under control and he can go back to chemo treatments in two weeks."

Virginia got up and gave Nate a hug. He didn't push her away, but he stood stiffly, accepting the embrace as if it was something a person had to endure. She wasn't offended— he was going through a tough time.

"It's hard," she said. "You should let some- one help you."

"I have a sister," Nate said. "She's only an hour away if I need her."

Henry distributed coffee to Alice and Vir- ginia and carefully peeled the white lid from his own. He sat at a side chair and crossed one leg over the other.

"Can we join the meeting?" Henry asked. "It's nice and warm in here."

"Sure. I can tell you all about next week- end's wedding," Alice said as she opened a folder and spread out the contents on her desk. "Classic autumn theme with dark red as the color. The wedding will take place in the hotel rotunda and the reception in the lobby. We can finally use that space now that the hotel is closed for the season."

Virginia remembered her wedding and honeymoon at the Lake Breeze Hotel more than thirty-five years ago. Her dress had puffy lace sleeves that exuded youth and op- timism. Owning an amusement park through- out their thirty years of marriage had kept them both young and happy, even though Ford was hiding a dark secret of stress and financial strain that contributed to his fatal heart attack.

"It's a second-time-around wedding," Alice continued. "I love those. I think it's nice they want to celebrate it here, and I don't expect any drama out of an older couple."

"Hey," Henry said. "Don't count us old folks out. We can cause drama if we want to."

Nate laughed. "Do you want to?"

Henry winked at Alice. "I'd rather have a good cup of coffee these days."

"I know the bride," Virginia said.

"You do?" Alice asked.

"Judy is a good friend of mine." Virginia paused and swallowed. She felt the attention of everyone in the room and wished she'd kept her mouth shut. She didn't want to talk about it, especially with Henry in the room. Knowing everyone was awaiting an explanation, Virginia shook her head and muttered, "I think she's making a mistake."

Alice sat back in her desk chair. "I've met both the bride and groom and they seem really happy to me."

"She hardly knows him. They just met last

year even though they've both lived in Bayside all their lives."

"It's a fairly large city," Nate said. "I'm sure there are plenty of people I've never met."

"But if they never met before, it seems logical they didn't have the same interests," Virginia insisted. "Right?" She knew she sounded unreasonable, but Judy had lost her husband about the same time Virginia had. They'd bonded as widows, poured their energy and time into volunteering. If Judy was moving on, did that mean she'd forgotten her husband? Was it so easy to replace someone?

"They must have found some common ground," Henry observed. Virginia kept her head down and fussed with a loose thread on her pants.

"So you must be planning to attend the wedding," Alice said. "I'll make sure I cover you with one of our seasonal employees."

Virginia nodded. "The bride actually asked me to be her stand-in matron of honor in case her sister can't get here from Arizona. I guess her sister takes care of her in-laws and they have health problems."

Alice's eyebrows were up and her mouth

open just enough to make it clear she was surprised.

I shouldn't have withheld this information so long. It makes it seem as if I have something to hide.

"That's wonderful," Alice said quickly. "How fun to be asked to stand up for your friend on her second time around."

"I was there the first time, too," Virginia said. "They got married in a church downtown the summer after I did. Her reception was in the park. It was a hot day, and we were all worried about the cake sliding right off the table." Virginia smiled, thinking about how that was their greatest worry at the time. "Her husband was a wonderful man. He was the superintendent of the water plant until he passed away."

"I hope her new husband will be wonderful, too," Alice said kindly. "Mike is retired from the county sheriff's office and he's a widower. He seems really nice."

"We'll see," Virginia said. "Of course I hope for the best for them."

Virginia had put down a "plus one" on the RSVP two months ago. She wasn't even sure she wanted to go to the wedding, but she'd thought she might ask one of her daughters to go with her if she did. Recently, she'd considered asking Henry, just as a friend, but now she felt foolish bringing it up. Especially since she hadn't mentioned it before, the wedding was coming up soon and Alice was almost certainly counting on Henry to help organize the event.

"I should have mentioned it sooner," Virginia said.

"Don't worry. We have some great seasonal staff still around," Alice said. "And I know they'll appreciate getting the hours, especially with the holidays coming."

Virginia focused on her hands and twisted her wedding band around her finger. Even after five years of widowhood, she'd never taken it off. Soon, Judy would have a new wedding band. Was it as easy as that?

"Let's talk about the Christmas weekends since we're all huddling here and avoiding the snow," Nate suggested. "We've been so wrapped up in the fall festival that I feel I hardly know what to expect from Santa and his elves."

Alice raised a shoulder and grinned. "Fine with me. The snow put me in the holiday spirit." She grabbed her mouse and scooted closer to her computer screen. "I can even put on Christmas music while we go over the plans if no one objects."

"No objection here," Henry said. "This will be the first Christmas I won't be on an airplane. I always volunteered to work the holidays since I didn't have a family."

"That was nice of you," Virginia said. She was glad the conversation had shifted away from her friend's wedding and the sensitive subject of second-chance romances. "I love Christmas. I always thought it would be fun to open Starlight Point for the holidays, but it's a risk Ford and I never worked ourselves up to take. All the planning and hiring it requires. My kids are braver than I am."

Alice turned the computer speakers on low and found an online channel with holiday music. "I hope the December weekends will be great," she said. "I don't know what I'm most excited about."

ALICE WONDERED WHY Nate had followed Henry into her office and why he had chosen to stay. He could have said a polite hello and retreated to his office with his coffee.

He could have claimed he had work to do, a believable excuse with Halloween over and Christmas coming fast. After missing several days of work to take care of his father, he was almost certainly behind.

But instead of making excuses, he appeared to be making himself comfortable in a chair near the door of her office. Even the subject of second-chance weddings hadn't driven him out into the cold. Was he lonely after spending days with his ill father? Alice wished she could give him a hug and offer to help as Virginia had, but she had ended any hope of a relationship like that the moment she'd put down her napkin and stood up at their rehearsal dinner.

That was the past, and the future plans of Starlight Point had a lot more potential. Alice was happy to run through exact details of the December weekend plans with her guests so she could think out loud. She had the ice rink, tree lot and Santa's arrival mostly figured out. Food service, sleigh rides and other activities were fairly solid.

She was interested in hearing Nate's plans for promotions—something she'd left to him and had not heard much about—and also getting a practical take on parking and logistics from Henry and Virginia. How many people could they reasonably expect? Would they be able to change plans on the fly to accommodate the unexpected, such as a bumper crowd or a surprise snowstorm?

She was halfway through her list of questions when her desk phone rang.

"Any chance you could come out to the parking lot?" Jack Hamilton asked. "I've got the guys from the ice rink company out here. I need help answering their questions because I know next to nothing about ice skating."

Although she didn't delight in a trip to the windy and snowy parking lot, Alice quickly agreed. "I can be there in just a few minutes."

"Thanks," Jack said on the other end of the line.

As she spoke on the phone, Henry, Virginia and Nate all gave her curious looks. She held up one finger as if to say she'd explain in a moment.

"Any chance you could track down Nate and bring him along?" Jack asked. "I've got the newspaper out here, too. They're looking for a story on the Christmas weekends. Can't believe they just showed up and thought they were going to get pictures."

"He's right here," Alice said. She looked at Nate as she spoke. He sat up straighter and cocked his head as if he was awaiting orders. *His dedication is commendable. I hope it includes freezing outside.*

"Good," Jack said, relief in his voice. "He can wrangle the reporters while I set up for the Winter Olympics out here."

"We'll hurry," Alice said, laughing. "And I like your idea for a sports competition. Maybe next year."

She hung up the phone.

"When I said my children were brave, I didn't know they were planning to host the Winter Olympics," Virginia said.

Alice laughed. "Not this year. That was Jack calling from the parking lot. We've got the ice rink company setting up and reporters from the *Bayside Times* crashing the party." She smiled. "Fun for all."

"We're driving out there, right?" Nate asked. "I didn't bring my cross-country skis."

"You've spent too much time in Florida," Alice said, shaking her head. She opened a closet door built into the wood paneling of her office. "There's an extra hat and scarf in here."

"You're prepared," Virginia said.

"I started here last January and learned my lesson fast. I was used to the wind off the bay because I grew up in Bayside, but this peninsula gets it from three sides." She handed the red wool scarf and hat to Nate. "You'll want these."

"You kids have fun," Virginia said. "I'm going to plead old age and take the rest of the day off."

"Me, too," Henry agreed.

Alice grabbed her car keys and a folder of plans from her desk. "We could share a ride," she suggested to Nate. She fully expected him to say no, even if it meant walking a mile to wherever his car was parked.

Nate pulled the red hat on and wrapped the scarf around his neck.

"Do I look like an elf on a mission?" he asked almost playfully. At least for him.

Alice laughed. "A very tall elf. I hope you get your picture in the paper looking like that. A color picture. It will be great advertising for Starlight Point's Christmas weekends."

Nate frowned and she thought he was

going to pull off the hat and scarf and chicken out on a trip outside. Instead, he squared his shoulders and stood stoically waiting, his PR neutral expression in place. Alice slipped on her wool coat and gloves and left the office with Nate right behind her.

"Speaking of advertising," Nate said as they walked down the hall. "I need to get started—probably yesterday. I wanted some photos of park visitors, but I may have to settle for staging the pictures."

"How will you do that?"

Nate shrugged. "I could get people to pose in front of decorations, maybe borrow some kids from other employees. The snow will help make the pictures attractive and realistic."

"It would be nice to get video of people on our skating rink," Alice suggested.

"Maybe you're right. Could you find some people and coach them? I've never skated."

Alice laughed. "Lots of people around here know how to ice skate. I'm surprised you don't. I hope the ice rink company can set it up and get it to freeze fast," she said, "so you can get promotional pictures soon."

Nate shivered and nodded. "Thanks."

Alice's car was parked just outside the gate nearest the corporate office. Nate used his gloved hand to wipe snow off her door handle and then the windshield. As Alice drove her small SUV on the outer loop road around Starlight Point, the windows started steaming up until Nate reached over and adjusted the defrost settings.

"Do you think Virginia would really skip her friend's wedding?" he asked.

Alice let out a long breath. "I wondered about that, too. I can't understand why Virginia never mentioned we were planning her friend's wedding—apparently a very close friend. It was odd."

"Her husband has been gone for a few years, right?"

"Virginia?" Alice asked. "About five, I think."

"So you might think she'd consider moving on herself."

"I couldn't say."

"I thought there might be a little something between Henry and Virginia," Nate commented. Alice negotiated a steep curve around the Wonderful West part of the peninsula. The waves from the lake and bay rolled in large angry-looking sweeps of blue, gray and green. It would be freezing cold in the parking lot.

"I noticed that, too."

"But if Virginia is adamantly opposed to her friend having a second chance at love, I guess she's already ruled it out for herself," Nate said.

Alice sighed. This talk of second chances was loaded, heavy with their own personal history and speculation about other people.

"I plan to talk to her about being her friend's matron of honor in case she's called upon. I can't imagine she'd turn down someone she's known for thirty years. How would her friend feel?"

Nate shrugged.

"Well I think her friend would feel terrible," Alice said. "She'd feel guilty about being happy, and no one should feel guilty about finding happiness. Everyone deserves it."

"Can't argue with that," Nate said. "You could talk to Virginia."

Alice laughed. "That worked out so well at the Halloween nightmare. And the more I think about it, the more I realize it was all my fault. I knew they were wrong for each other. It was obvious at every meeting and planning session we had. I should have told them."

"You can't tell people those things."

"Why not? If being honest avoids bigger mistakes, maybe we have a moral obligation to speak up. It might have helped work out their problems before they destroyed their big day."

If only she'd been honest with herself and put the brakes on wedding planning long enough to evaluate whether or not marriage was something she and Nate were ready for. Had he really never seen it coming?

"You tried to do the right thing, and I respect that," he said. "But sometimes brutal honesty is just brutal, nothing more."

CHAPTER FOURTEEN

REHEARSAL DINNERS ARE *not my favorite*, Alice thought. She loved weddings. Planning the music, flowers, vows, colors and food were the fun parts of beginning a life together. Nothing made her happier than going to the florist's shop with a bride to decide on daisies or roses. Even though she'd imagined herself planning other special events, her time at Starlight Point had made her love the moment when the bride walked down the aisle to join the waiting groom. Her heart lifted with each step the bride and her party took, and she adored seeing the groom's expression of wonder.

She had never given Nate an opportunity to have that look. Knowing how carefully he reserved his feelings, would he have given his heart away with his expression?

The night before the wedding when the party gathered to begin the official transformation of bride and groom to husband and wife should be a happy time of waiting, like Christmas Eve. But to Alice, it brought back the night before her own wedding when she had finally gathered the courage to say no.

"You can't believe how surprised I am to be here," Henry said, leaning close to Alice as she watched the guests arriving and finding their seats.

She turned and found Henry wearing a dark suit with a burgundy tie. "You look dangerously handsome."

Henry pulled at his tie. "I swore I'd never wear a tie again after I retired from the airline."

"Virginia must have been very convincing when she asked you to dress up and be her date."

"Yes, but she asked me at the last minute, which isn't too flattering. Maybe everyone else turned her down."

Alice smiled. "You know that's not true. Tonight is also the early Thanksgiving feast for employees in the ballroom, so she was probably thinking of going to that instead. That's where the rest of her family is. She wasn't committed to attending this wedding until recently, and she was probably being courteous to you by not dragging you into her indecision."

"I wouldn't have minded. What I'd like to know is how you convinced her to come to this wedding."

Alice shrugged. "It wasn't the hardest thing I've done all summer. She needed an impartial person to talk to. Her own children are too close to the situation."

"She could have talked to me."

"You," Alice said, shaking her head and pointing playfully at Henry, "are definitely too close to the situation."

"How's that?"

Alice had said too much. She wanted to be truthful and tell Henry that his company was the reason Virginia was so conflicted about her friend getting married. He had to see it for himself already. If other widows in Virginia's circle of friends could find love a second time around, it made it even more plausible and frightening for Virginia.

"You should take your seat at the head table." Alice pointed toward the long table where the bride, groom and bridal party were seated.

"I don't really belong there since I just met the bride today."

"You're there for Virginia, just keep that in mind. She needs a nice steady rock like you right now."

"Thanks. Every man loves being labeled nice and steady." Henry laughed. "I'm glad to say it's not the worst thing I've ever been called."

Henry strode to the table of honor and took his seat next to Virginia. He exuded confidence in everything he did, and Alice could easily imagine him at the controls of a passenger jet. The big question was how he would navigate his relationship with Virginia. Alice knew from her conversation with Virginia that she liked Henry enough for it to worry her. Having lost someone she loved very much, she wasn't sure she could take a chance on someone new.

The rehearsal dinner began with a brief toast from the bride's son and the groom's daughter. Unlike weddings of young people, the toast did not include slanderous stories of wild bachelor days. Instead, the family members of the soon-to-be husband and wife expressed simple joy at their parents' happiness.

When the bride stood up to speak, the entire restaurant fell silent. Alice's chest flared with pain and she struggled to draw a breath. What was the bride going to say?

She vividly remembered the stunned silence after she'd stood at her rehearsal dinner and quietly told the assembled friends and family that she had changed her mind and would not be marrying Nate Graham. What had Nate thought at the time? She regretted that she would never know. He didn't fight, didn't risk a scene. Simply stared coldly as she walked out.

In the hours, days and weeks that had followed, Alice had expected him to show up on her doorstep demanding an explanation, even fighting to get her back. Instead, silence. Was he secretly glad she called it off and she was the one who looked like the bad guy? She remembered his face whenever she'd said *I love you*. He always responded appropriately, saying the three little words cautiously. *Who says I love you cautiously, even if it is most dangerous sentence in the world?*

"Thank you for coming this evening," the bride said. Alice waited, intent on every word. "Getting married at our ages is not the same as getting married when you're twenty or twenty-five. At that age, you have no idea what life is going to throw at you, but you're darn sure you can face it if you just have love."

The silver-haired bride paused, and Alice watched Virginia's expression. She looked as if she was witnessing something painful but was helpless to do anything about it. Was she hoping her friend would change her mind, even at the last moment?

"Believe me, I'm sure we've both had second thoughts, even wondered what possessed us to fall in love when we were least expecting it." She turned to her intended groom and put a hand on his shoulder. A flash went off and Alice followed the bright trail back to the man holding the camera.

Nate, wearing his PR neutral smile.

He caught Alice's eye and they stood frozen in the bizarre experience of listening to a bride at a rehearsal dinner express honest feelings about second thoughts. Nate's expression hardened and he looked away. Alice swallowed the lump in her throat and focused on the beautiful bride who was twice as brave as Alice for going through with two weddings in one lifetime.

"But loving someone is worth risking everything. So thank you to everyone for joining us. Especially to my dear friend Virginia who has always stood by my side and is standing in tomorrow for my sister who wasn't able to get here from Arizona. Mike and I want to express our love and gratitude to our children and extended family for welcoming our decision to get married."

Alice released the breath she'd been holding.

The bride raised her glass. "To the future."

As guests lifted their glasses, Alice stole a look at Virginia. Her glass hovered in the air and she exchanged a quick glance with Henry before sipping the champagne.

"To the future," Alice whispered. She risked a glance and discovered Nate was gone. He'd taken a good picture for his blog and then taken off as fast as he could go.

As soon as she could slip away, Alice left the marina restaurant, swung through the open park gate and crossed the wide midway to the ballroom. She was starving after a long day. The turkey, stuffing, mashed potatoes and pies she'd seen on the menu for the employee dinner were calling her name. As she approached the ballroom, a tall man exited through the glass doors.

"Nate," Alice said, halting his movement. What could she say after that rehearsal dinner had chafed so many old wounds. She hadn't asked him if he planned to attend the employee party, and now she wondered why he was leaving right after he'd gotten there. "You're already leaving?"

He nodded. "I only stopped by for a while. I didn't want to be unfriendly or ungrateful to the Hamiltons. I love this job. But I have a…family thing…tonight."

"Your dad?"

Nate nodded. If she had married him, they would be talking about her father-in-law and sharing the burden of caring for a loved one. But when she'd rejected Nate, she'd also rejected his family. Did his father face cancer with a neutral *everything's fine* expression? Is that where Nate had learned to mask his feelings and soldier through life?

Nate cleared his throat. "I don't like leaving him alone any more than I have to." He held up a bag filled with foam takeout containers. "The food inside looks terrific, and I'm headed home to share it with him."

"I'll be thinking of you." Alice put a hand on Nate's shoulder, almost expecting him to brush it off. Instead, he pulled her into a long wordless hug.

Having Nate's arms around her made the entire Starlight Point midway slip away, as if they were standing on an island. The intimacy brought every one of her feelings to the surface, and she pulled away from him, intending to finally have the honest conversation they both needed.

She was ready to tell him it was time to dig up old feelings, but when she saw his face, she stopped. His lip quivered a little, but his face was still pulled into a calm expression as if hugging his ex-fiancée on a darkened midway didn't move him at all.

What would?

He walked away a moment later without a word, and Alice pictured him getting into his car—a dark blue sedan—and driving across the Point Bridge. Alone, physically and emotionally.

Alice shoved through the ballroom door into cheerful lighting, music and the tantalizing aroma of good food. *Such a contrast.* She picked up a white china plate from the end of a long table covered with silver chafing dishes and started down the line with every intention of heaping her plate full. It was the only way she could fill the empty space left from her encounter with Nate.

"Over here," June called when Alice got to the end of the line. June half stood and waved.

Alice strode over to June's table and plunked down her plate on the bright red tablecloth. "Getting a drink. Be right back."

She walked past sparkling red punch bowls. A variety of mini cans of sodas on ice. Pitchers of water and iced tea. All lovely, but Alice went for the waiting bartender who only had one question. "Red or white?"

"I think it's an occasion for red," Alice said.

She balanced her full glass of red wine and walked carefully back to the table.

"How is our mother behaving?" June asked. "My sister and I have been wondering." Evie was just down the table with her husband, but she was talking to someone else. Alice noticed she had a glass of water instead of wine, and Evie glowed with happiness. She wished she could have been there for the weddings of the three Hamiltons that had taken place three years in a row. June had shown her pictures, knowing her love of big events. They were all beautiful but different, and everyone in the Hamilton family seemed so happy. What about Virginia? She deserved a happy ending, too.

"When I left the rehearsal dinner, she was playing poker with the best man and knocking back shots of Jack Daniels," Alice joked, trying to put June at ease.

June grinned. "Good. I was afraid she wasn't going to have fun. She's taking her friend's wedding much too seriously. Sheesh," June said, leaning back in her chair, "you'd think she was the one getting married."

Alice cocked her head but didn't comment.

"What?" June asked. "You have that look you get when you want to tell someone exactly what you think but you're too nice. I've seen you use it at least twelve times this summer."

"I'm not too nice," Alice said. "It's just that sometimes the absolute truth does more harm than good."

"Hard to believe," Mel said. He had liberated a bottle of wine from the bar and refilled his glass and his wife's. He set the bottle in the middle of the table.

"What do you want to tell me about my mother?" June pressed.

"Nothing you don't already know."

When June was silent, Mel filled in the gaps. "Virginia is having a little fling with a seasonal employee. We've all been there."

"Enough wine for you," June said.

"This is a nice party," Alice said. She forked a piece of turkey and enjoyed it slowly instead of being drawn into June's questioning. The gravy was heavenly and its flavor warmed Alice as she surveyed the room. Although Starlight Point employed two thousand seasonal employees for the summer months, the year-round staff was much smaller. Numbering only about a hundred, they were a close-knit family.

"I wish Nate could have stayed," June said. "He seems to like it here, and he's done a great job with our media presence. Almost as if it's an obsession with him to be everywhere at once covering everything."

Was it an obsession? Alice had noticed him

at every event she'd planned. He was always present taking pictures, making notes and turning his observations into blogs, articles and teasers on social media. What drove him? Alice knew he loved Starlight Point because he'd loved visiting there frequently as a teenager and college student—with her.

And even though she was certain of his affection and loyalty for his employer, she knew there was something he loved even more. The business of appearances. The life of Nate Graham…where everything's just fine.

CHAPTER FIFTEEN

"YOUR SISTERS ARE both coming home for Thanksgiving next week." Alice's mother poured water into the coffee maker as the morning sun lit the kitchen counter.

"I'm looking forward to it." Alice hadn't seen her sisters since her dad's fiftieth birthday party in August. Always close growing up, they'd called and texted throughout the fall, but it would be nice to catch up. Should she say anything about working with her former fiancé? If anyone would understand, it would be Mallory and Lauren, but they might also ask questions she didn't know how to answer.

"Mallory's bringing Todd," her mom continued. "Lauren's whole family is coming, of course." Twin daughters and a son kept Alice's older sister busy. She was only twenty-nine, but she already had an entire family. Not that Alice was jealous. She loved seeing her nieces and nephew, and she hoped they could come again to go ice skating and visit with Santa at Starlight Point's winter festival.

Alice got three coffee cups out of the cabinet and lined them up. Her father would be down to eat any moment before leaving for the bank. Although her father always wore a jacket and tie that suited his profession, Alice's mother was a much more colorful dresser.

Her mother owned a clothing store in downtown Bayside specializing in actual vintage clothing and new clothing that appeared old. Her favorite time periods were the 1930s and 1940s. When Alice was a teenager, she would race home to help in her mother's store, loving the colors and patterns and the excitement of opening boxes.

"Is that new?" Alice asked, pointing to her mother's vintage polka dot skirt in red and ivory.

Her mother fingered the cotton fabric. "It's one of our new lines in time for Christmas. We got them in winter colors this time around—you should see the dark green one— but I'm going to put in an order for spring and summer. People like the dots, I think."

"I love it. Will you order in pink ones for me?"

Her mother smiled and shook her head. "You shouldn't let your aunt get to you. My sister has been bossy and opinionated her entire life. When she told you redheads couldn't wear pink when you were in kindergarten, I'm sure she had no idea it would scar you for life."

"It didn't. I wear pink almost every day."

"That's not exactly what I meant. You're quite a lot like her in the way you tell people the truth whether they want to hear it or not."

"It's better than pretending, and you never have to wonder what I'm thinking."

"Just don't tell women what they can and can't wear or what they should do with their makeup or hair. It becomes baggage."

"Uh-oh," Alice said. "I may have rained on my coworker's idea of getting highlights."

"When are you going to learn?" her mother asked.

Alice's phone buzzed in the purse she'd slung over the back of a kitchen chair. She dug it out and looked at the caller identification. Nate? He hadn't been to work in three days, and she'd assumed he was taking care of his father after another round of chemo. Alice had been torn about what to do or say. She couldn't stop by the hospital or his house with flowers as she might with another co-worker's relative. Instead, she had texted Nate and simply said she wished him well. It was skimpy, but it was all she could do.

"Hello, Nate?" she answered, a question in her voice.

Alice's mother raised an eyebrow as she paused the coffee maker and poured a cup for her father, who had just come into the kitchen. Alice felt like a teenager trying to talk to her boyfriend on the phone while both parents listened in, and she was tempted to leave the room. But that was silly. She was a grown woman answering a call from a co-worker.

"Alice," he said. There was a long pause. She assumed he was gathering his thoughts, but wouldn't he have done that before he called? Maybe it was terrible news and he was steadying his nerves.

"Can I help you with something? I hope your father is better."

"He's hanging in there."

"I'm glad. Can I do…anything for you?"

"I'm calling about work."

Of course he was. Their relationship was all about Starlight Point. It had to be.

"Video," he continued. "I've gotten behind, and the Christmas weekends open soon."

"Okay, I could try to take some video of the decorations that are finished, maybe record some of the preparations like the big garlands going up?"

"That's not what I was thinking."

Alice sat at the chair her father pulled out for her. Her mother put a cup of coffee in front of her and took her father by the arm, pulling him out of the room. Did her parents really think this was a personal call? They knew she worked with Nate, but they had reserved comment and asked few questions.

"Tell me what you're thinking," she said.

"Ice skating. Henry told me the rink is solid."

"We could get some employees and maybe their kids to try it out so you can take a video."

"I was thinking of you," Nate said, his words slow and deliberate.

I was thinking of you, too.

"If you put on that red scarf and hat that I

still have, maybe something green to go with it…" he suggested.

"You think I could skate around the rink, and you could record me with the roller coaster hills of Starlight Point in the background."

"Yes."

"Why does it have to be me?" Alice asked.

Nate paused for several seconds. "I want it to be great. Sure I can edit it on my computer, but if I start with a beautiful skater… it will make my job a lot easier."

Alice hesitated. When he said beautiful skater, did he mean her skating was beautiful or she was?

"I can use all the help I can get right now," Nate said.

Alice heard the pain in his voice. Was it his father's illness or the fact that he had to ask someone for help? Exposing his vulnerability was a gauntlet of fire for Nate. She had struggled to understand exactly what drove them apart five years ago but now, every time she saw his PR neutral face, she was putting the pieces together. Something had made him very afraid to open his heart, and she knew it wasn't because she'd left him at the altar.

That was a result, not a cause. What was the cause?

Whatever the reason, he needed help now, and Alice wanted Starlight Point to have a successful Christmas festival. "I'll grab my skates and meet you there in an hour."

"Thanks. You're really getting me out of a bind, and I…."

She waited for him to finish the sentence but decided to help him with that, too. "See you soon," she said, ending the conversation.

Alice dropped her phone in her purse and walked to the living room, where her parents were having coffee on the couch. "Did you tell me you had a dark green polka dot skirt in your store?"

Her mother nodded. "Are we going shopping?"

"Speed shopping. I just agreed to put on my skates and do a promotional video for Starlight Point on our temporary ice rink."

Her mother jumped up. "I've got a vintage dark green velvet jacket in a size four. It's a perfect complement to the skirt."

"I hope you don't mind opening your shop an hour early today."

"For you, anything," her mother said.

As they headed into the kitchen, Alice turned to her dad. "Would you mind if I borrowed your skates, too? Just in case I can rope a man into skating with me?"

"Take them, and good luck," her father said, smiling over his morning coffee.

"CAN WE MOVE those evergreen trees over here to make a nice background?" Nate asked the men who were completing the setup of the ice rink.

"You want more evergreens?" a voice behind him asked. "I can put you to work unloading the truck." Nate turned and found Mel Preston dressed in his usual maintenance blues with a blue winter coat and Starlight Point ski cap. Mel grinned and jerked his thumb at a panel truck behind him where Henry and other workers were busy. "We could use the help."

"I'll just put my camera in my car," Nate said.

Glad to have something physical to take his mind off the nervous energy thrumming through his body, Nate shed the camera and pulled on a pair of leather gloves. While he waited for Alice to arrive, he made trip after trip from the truck to the ice rink carrying heavy potted evergreens and arranging them where Henry instructed. The diagram in Henry's hands flapped in the November breeze.

It was good weather for shooting video. Slightly overcast, but still bright. The ice rink had a red fence around it, and with evergreens in groups, it was a perfect holiday scene. Another truck arrived with props from the storage area at Starlight Point. Nate was sweating inside his winter coat as he helped unload big boxes covered in colorful plastic giftwrap that would withstand a month of winter weather.

With the giftwrapped boxes and trees, the holiday wonderland was complete. All he needed now was his ice skater.

Not *his* ice skater. Was it a mistake to ask Alice for a favor? He hadn't seen her in days, and he'd had plenty of time to think as he'd sat keeping watch over his dad, making him food, finding his favorite shows on television.

A flash of sun off a windshield alerted him to a car arriving. He pulled off his winter coat and tucked it in the front seat of his car as Alice pulled in next to him. Nate grabbed his camera.

"Have you worked up a sweat skating already?" she asked.

He shook his head. "Working. I unloaded evergreens and decorations for the last half hour." He hated to admit how much he'd enjoyed the physical labor. Being outside in the fresh air made him feel alive. Alice's fresh face had the same effect. When he was with her, he felt younger—as if he'd gone back five years. *Young and foolish*, he reminded himself.

"Sorry. I tried to hurry."

"No criticism intended," Nate said, smiling. "You dressed the part." He gestured to her green velvet jacket and long green skirt with white polka dots. "The video should be great."

"I just need a few warmup laps," Alice said. "I haven't skated since last winter."

"It'll come back to you, right, like riding a bicycle?"

"Yes." She reached into the back seat of her car and pulled out a pair of black men's skates. "These are a size twelve. Any chance they'll fit you?"

Nate had worn a size twelve since sophomore year of high school. He'd bet his life Alice knew it at the time and still remembered. Nate shivered at the thought. Maybe he should get his coat out of his car. "They may fit," he said, "but I've never ice skated in my life."

"I tried to teach you."

Nate remembered that day vividly. One of their high school friends had lived on a cove along the lake, and the shallow water froze enough to skate on. There had been a bonfire on the shore and a large group of their friends gathered around. It was right after Christmas three years after they graduated from high school. Some friends were home from college and some were moving on with their lives in other ways, getting married or moving away to start new jobs. Nate remembered thinking he needed to do something to show he was growing up and changing, too. It had been later that night that he'd proposed.

"Remember?" Alice prompted.

"I know, but I wasn't ready to learn then."

"Maybe it's not too late," Alice said.

Nate sucked in a breath of cold air. "Alice, do you really think I can learn to ice skate?"

She cocked her head and just enough sun broke through the clouds to highlight her auburn hair. It was one of the first times he'd seen her wearing no pink at all, except in her cheeks colored by the November breeze.

"I believe it depends upon the quality of the teacher and the motivation of the student. I know at least one of those is solid."

Nate laughed. "Tell you what, let me get my video first. That way, in case I break one arm or both arms, I'll still have good advertising for Starlight Point."

"It's a deal. Just tell me what you want, and I'll make it happen."

Nate knew what he needed in a promotional video, but he never took time to think about what *he* really wanted. To want something was to open a door into your heart others might see. There was a time when he'd believed having Alice would make him happy, but then she'd broken his heart with no warning and walked out of his life.

Alice raised a brow and waited. "I'll take a few laps and get the feel of the ice while you think about it," she suggested.

She slung her skates over her shoulder with a move that suggested long practice. He was definitely out of his league here. He waited while she sat on one of the many benches alongside the temporary rink and laced up. Her long red-brown hair fell over the shoulder of her green velvet jacket. She was beautiful. She had hardly changed since he'd first kissed her by her locker junior year.

Well, her appearance hadn't changed, but had she? There was no safe way to find out, even if he wanted to know the answer.

She stepped onto the ice and began moving with sweeping, graceful steps, lapping the sizable rink in only seconds.

With plenty of space to spare in the massive parking lot, Starlight Point had gone big with the rink. They still had plenty of parking spaces, since the crowd of locals who would show up for wintry weekends was considerably smaller than the summer estimates of guests traveling from all over the Midwest.

Nate leaned on the rail to steady himself as he followed Alice with his camera. Starlight Point's roller coasters towered behind her as she executed a spin without losing any speed. She flashed past the evergreens and sparkling packages, her long skirt and hair flowing. *Perfect.* All he needed to do was edit in Christmas music, and this video would have every family in the Bayside area coming out to experience an old-fashioned holiday.

After five minutes of her skating, Nate had all the video he truly needed, but watching her made his heart light. With every quick turn and spin she made and each light leap, he felt his worries melting away. If only he could move like that, with such freedom, as if no one was watching or judging.

As Alice passed in front of him, she smiled and waved without slowing down.

Henry put his forearms on the rail next to Nate. "This will make a beautiful advertisement."

"It certainly will. Can't believe how lucky we are that Alice was a junior champion skater."

"She's full of surprises."

Nate nodded. If only Henry knew how true that was.

"I wonder if Virginia skates? Funny how you can spend hours and days with someone and there are still things you don't have the first clue about."

"You could ask her," Nate suggested.

Henry shook his head. "I don't know. Sometimes I feel I'm being invited into her confidence and sometimes I think she's looking for bricks to build a wall."

"Walls have their merits."

Alice skidded to a stop in front of them, throwing ice over their shoes. "Ready for your turn?"

"I'm out," Henry said. "I'm on the clock."

"We could call it work," Alice said. "A handsome man like you holding hands with me as we skate would make great video."

Henry laughed. "We'd look like a father and daughter."

"So?"

"That's not a bad idea, getting someone else out there on the ice with Alice," Nate said.

"You're right." Henry held out his hand for Nate's camera. "I think I have a better chance taking video than I do out there on the ice. You're thirty years younger than I am, so you're on deck."

Alice flashed a huge smile at Nate. "Ready when you are."

He handed Henry his camera and sat on the bench. As he took off his shoes and stuck his feet in the unfamiliar skates, he explained how to work the video mode on the camera and what kind of shots would be most useful for publicity and web video. Alice skated a few more laps while she waited.

"You're assuming you'll be on your feet swirling around this rink next to Alice," Henry said. "You must have some experience skating."

"Not one single bit, but lately I've been challenging myself to try things even though I feel like I'm on thin ice."

Henry laughed. "I'll be ready to call the paramedics."

Alice stopped by the rail. "I'd advise you to tie those skates really tight, it'll keep your ankles from wobbling."

Nate pulled up his jeans and tightened the laces while Alice put an elbow on the rail and watched. "Have you really never been on the ice? Not even…since…?"

"Never," he said quickly. "Any pointers?"

"Keep a slight bend in your knees, put your weight in your thighs and keep your back straight. Let yourself glide. Trust yourself."

Nate got up and, keeping one hand firmly on the railing, took a step onto the ice. With the skates on, he was well over six feet and the ice looked far away. *This is going to hurt.* Alice took his arm. Although she was a foot shorter than he was, her grip on his arm was steadying.

"You can do this, just take short steps until you're more comfortable."

Nate took his hand off the railing and held it out to his side for balance. He made a short, wobbly sweep of his right foot and followed with his left.

"Nice," Alice said. "Back straight."

Nate had played basketball throughout high school and on an intramural league in college, so he had some balance and strength. He tried to channel the athleticism he'd let lapse in the past few years as he'd concentrated on his career and keeping his life together. *Trust yourself and take a chance.*

He tried a few more glides and stayed on his feet. Concentrating on the ice right in front of him, he was afraid to look up. He hoped the skaters who visited were more confident than he was so they could appreciate the location and the Christmas decorations. What good would the scenery be if people only stared at their skates in desperation? They'd miss the most beautiful part.

"I wish the speakers for the music were functioning," Alice said. "Music makes skating a lot more fun."

Nate bobbled and caught himself. "I don't think I could handle the distraction."

"You could. It would take your mind off the fear of falling."

Fear of falling. That was a feeling Nate knew very well. He risked a glance to his side. Alice's cheeks were pink and her eyes bright. With a shock, he realized he was in grave danger of falling for her. Again.

He pulled his arm free.

"Are you ready to try this on your own?" she asked.

He nodded, keeping his attention straight ahead. As he tried several awkward steps and repeated the movement, Alice stayed right by his side. When he gained confidence enough to lengthen his strides, Alice moved out in front and skated backward so she could watch him.

"Show off," he said.

She laughed. "I'm just trying to encourage you."

They made it halfway around the rink and Nate remembered Henry with the camera.

He wasn't taking video of this, was he? Nate halted by the rail and glanced across the ice. Henry sat on the bench with the camera beside him. Good.

"Enjoying the show," Henry yelled. "Waiting for you to get good at this."

"Got all day?"

"If we hold hands, would you feel braver?" Alice asked. "We might even complete a lap."

"Sounds like a challenge." And a very bad idea. They'd held hands at football games, the movies, between classes and on long walks on cold nights.

It had all ended with her giving back his ring and refusing his hand in marriage.

Nate took a deep breath and took Alice's hand. It was the only way he was going to make it around the rink and provide decent video for the advertisement he desperately needed to create.

They both wore thin gloves, but he felt the warmth of her slender fingers anyway. He found a bit of rhythm as they skated together. *Dangerous rhythm*. Gained confidence and something resembling speed. *Too fast*. He waved to Henry as they passed by. It made him temporarily lose his balance and sway, but Alice let go of his hand and grabbed his arm to steady him. He didn't fall.

As they skated, haltingly on his part and gracefully on hers, a lap around the rink, Nate caught a glimpse of Henry with the camera raised. He had to make this look good. He stood straighter and smiled at Alice. Just a happy couple skating away at Starlight Point. She caught his glance and smiled back. Her hand in his felt as if it belonged there. Maybe there was a chance for them again. Did Alice feel the same way? Her eyes practically danced. Was it for him, or was it the joy of skating?

Nate lost his fear of falling for just a moment as he looked into Alice's eyes, and that's when he lost control. The world spun, and he let go of Alice's hand so he wouldn't pull her down with him. He tried to tuck his head and arms for impact, but it didn't help.

Ice is hard.

Nate opened his eyes. Alice hovered over him, her brows together and mouth forming an open circle.

"Are you okay?"

"I think so." He had to put on a brave face no matter how he felt.

She extended a hand and pulled him to his knees. As he tried to stand, she put her arms around him to steady him.

"This is the hardest part," she said. "Getting back up when you fall."

She kept her arms around him for a moment more. As he struggled to his feet, breathless and disoriented, he was also strangely happy. He looked down at Alice and fought the impulse to hold her close and kiss her. Her lips parted and her eyes widened. Was she thinking the same thing?

Nate swallowed. "I think my skating lesson is over for the day."

She nodded and turned, still holding onto his arm. "Only half a lap to the bench."

They skated together, haltingly, to the gate where Henry waited with the camera.

"I got the whole thing recorded," Henry said. "You two will be immortalized."

CHAPTER SIXTEEN

"Is it cheating to start our Christmas shopping before Thanksgiving?" June asked.

"All the shops are decorated," Virginia said as they walked together in downtown Bayside, "and we're not the only ones getting ahead of the season."

"You're right. Evie already finished hers. She had it on a spreadsheet."

"My Christmas list keeps getting longer," Virginia said. "I should have started shopping a month ago." She put an arm around her daughter. "You know what's strange for me? Seeing Starlight Point decorated for Christmas. Garlands on the carousel horses, red and green lights in all the trees, shops and restaurants with their windows painted. I can't believe we never did it before."

"A lot of those ideas came from Alice. She has enough imagination for five people."

Virginia stopped walking in front of a

men's store. A sweater in the window would be a perfect gift for a man with gray eyes and just a little silver hair at his temples. June gave her a curious look, but Virginia wasn't ready to share her thoughts. Instead, she opened her purse and dug through it for her list.

She gripped the paper with both hands as it flapped in the wind off the bay and read the names aloud. "Jack, Augusta, Nora, June, Mel, Ross, Abigail, Evie, Scott and their baby—won't we know soon if it's a boy or girl?"

"Ultrasound next month, I think," June said. "What did you write next to my name? Something fabulous, I hope. You always give the best gifts."

"Caroline and her husband, Matt," Virginia continued, concealing the paper from June, "I consider them part of the family now."

"Me, too. How about Henry?"

Virginia glanced up. Had June noticed her looking at the gray wool sweater?

"Henry," June repeated. "You know what I'm talking about. He's on your list, right?"

"Of course we always do something special for the people who work for us, especially the ones who stick around when the weather gets cold."

"That's not what I mean," June said. "Henry doesn't just work for Starlight Point. You two are…friends."

Virginia didn't say anything. Of course they were friends. Her children and everyone else who worked at Starlight Point knew that. They were coworkers who trusted each other's judgment. Brought each other food and drinks when the day got long. He had a key to her home in case she needed someone to run over and let Gladys out when she wasn't available.

That was a friendly relationship, wasn't it?

Virginia started walking. "Your father and I used to come downtown to do all our Christmas shopping. That was before people ordered everything online. We'd leave you kids with my mother and try to get it all done in one day. Except the gifts we got for each other, of course."

"Shopping is always fun," June agreed. "But Christmas shopping is the best."

"While we were gone, my mother would let the three of you decorate the tree so we'd be surprised every year when we came home."

"I remember that," June said. "We always thought we were genuinely surprising you."

Virginia laughed. "You used to put so many icicles on our tree. It was the gaudiest thing."

"But sparkly," June protested.

"Jack thought the higher branches were his territory and he'd load them up with bulbs. It was a miracle it didn't tip over. And Evie would put all her ornaments on in perfect lines so it was symmetrical and balanced. She liked it to be mathematical."

"No surprise there. I'm sure she still does that," June said, laughing. "I hope Scott doesn't mind."

"I don't know about that, but she did tell me he won't have a live Christmas tree in the house. He made her buy a flame retardant fake one."

June shrugged. "I guess firefighters see hazards everywhere. Especially Scott. Imagine what he'll be like when their baby comes. He probably won't even let his kids have candles on their birthday cakes."

Virginia laughed. "I bet he'll be okay. He and Caroline have both finally put their pasts behind them, losing their sister in that fire. It's nice seeing them both happy."

"Second chances," June said. She paused in front of a children's clothing store. "Want to help me pick out a Christmas dress for Abigail?"

"I'd love to."

Virginia and June sorted through holiday dresses as the sun streamed through the wide store windows. Like many of the shops at street level, this one had a long history. Its floor was made up of tiny tiles arranged in a pattern and bearing the name of the original owners of the building, Chase and Mackert. The heavy front doors had brass handles, and merchandise was arranged under a high ornate ceiling.

After much deliberation, June held up her two final choices—a deep rose dress with a smocked bodice and satin skirt and a red velvet dress with sequins in a diamond pattern on the skirt. "Which one?" she asked her mother.

Virginia smiled. "You and Evie had matching dresses one year with smocked bodices."

"I remember those dresses," June said, nodding. "Maybe that's why I like this one."

June held the deep rose one higher than the other.

"Decision made," Virginia said.

"Should I text Augusta and see if she wants me to get one for Nora, too? Matching cousins?"

"They have plenty of them. Maybe you could show it to her when you're all over for Thanksgiving and she can decide."

June paid for the dress at the old-fashioned counter and waited while the clerk zipped it into a weatherproof bag. When they left the shop, Alice was nearby, just leaving her mother's clothing store.

"Hello," Alice said as they came under the shadow of the awning. She wore a gray wool coat with a pink and gray plaid scarf. She gestured toward their bags. "Christmas shopping?"

June nodded. "Getting a head start before we start cooking for Thanksgiving."

"My mother is in pre-Thanksgiving mode. She dug out all the fancy plates and silverware and they're stacked and ready. My sisters are coming home so she's also in full mom mode."

"Your mom's store is one of my favorites," June said.

"Want to see the new clothes she has in the shop? I already took a green dotted skirt and velvet jacket off the rack."

"I saw that," June said. "In the video promotion for the Winter Weekends. It was perfect with the ice skates, like an advertisement for a good old-fashioned holiday."

"That was the idea. I haven't seen the video yet. Did it happen to include any bloopers? Perhaps of Nate flailing on the ice?"

June shook her head. "He must have edited that part out. It was all you. With your wonderful red hair and that green outfit—not to mention your ability to skate—you'll have families coming to our rink from all over Michigan."

"I'm glad we invested in a big stock of rental skates, then."

"I have my own skates," June said. "I'm not a bad skater because I had years of dance lessons. But apparently Nate thought you'd make a prettier picture."

"Ha!" Alice laughed. "I was only his first choice because he knew I was a junior skater."

"You and Nate both grew up in Bayside. Did you know each other before you ended up working together?" Virginia asked. The tension she'd noticed between them had to come from somewhere, and June had told her about the day Alice and Nate had met in the Lake Breeze Hotel lobby. They couldn't agree on whether they already knew each other.

"We went to high school together," Alice said. She turned away and peered in the front window of her mother's shop, giving someone an exaggerated wave. In the window's reflection, Virginia saw Alice's strained expression, but when Alice turned back to them she had a bright smile. Nate used a smile just like that when he was dealing with the press. Maybe the two of them had something in common but didn't want to talk about it.

"Go ahead and look in the vintage shop," she said to both girls. "I saw something in the men's store across the street I might pick up for...someone special."

June grinned at her mother. "Come find us when you're done. I'll probably be in the dressing room trying to decide between three things I love."

"Give yourself a break and get all three," Virginia said. "Blame it on the holidays."

ALICE OPENED THE closet door slowly. She knew what was on the other side. Her sisters would be home soon for Thanksgiving, and it was time for the shaming routine of moving her unused wedding dress to her own closet while the spare bedroom was in use. How many Thanksgivings, Christmases and other visits had come and gone in the five years since she'd decided not to put on that dress and marry Nate?

Too many.

She held it by the silver hanger. In all the years she'd been moving it, she had never unzipped the opaque bag. It was as if she was hiding a crime. She hung it on the outside of the closet door and waited for the usual feeling of how she had disappointed everyone to wash over her.

It didn't.

The only person she had truly disappointed was herself, and she had learned a lot in the hard days and months following what was supposed to be the happiest day of her life. She'd learned to listen to her heart and tell the truth to everyone—starting with herself. Seeing Nate again with his guarded expression and factory smile reiterated those feelings that drove her to tears, even on the day before their wedding.

She unzipped the bag a few inches until the white satin edge of the bodice appeared. Even though she hadn't laid eyes on the gown in years, she remembered every detail. Alice pulled the zipper down some more and realized she was looking at the back of the dress. Satin-covered buttons that hid a zipper brushed her fingers as she unzipped the bag more. The heavy train that someone—her mother?—had carefully folded was bulging against the garment bag. When she unzipped it all the way to the bottom, the train cascaded out and tickled her bare feet.

Alice pushed the bag off the shoulders of the dress and flipped it around so she could face it for the first time since she was twenty-two. It didn't hurt. It didn't kill her. It was just a dress. And she had almost saved enough cash to repay her parents for it and the other wasted fanfare of her wedding.

Did the dress still fit? Alice crossed the small bedroom and closed the door. She slid out of her sweater and jeans guiltily, as if she were borrowing something without permission. She unzipped the gown and slipped into it. In the full-length mirror on the wall next to the closet, she watched herself become, in appearance, a bride. Shoulders in place, bodice adjusted and back zipper done up only halfway because she couldn't reach far enough to do it herself, the dress still fit. She smiled at her reflection, twisted her hair up and held it with one hand on top of her head.

She heard a gasp and spun around. Her mother stood in the doorway, her hand on the doorknob. Her eyes were huge and she brought her other hand over her mouth.

"You caught me," Alice said, laughing. "Do I look ridiculous?"

"You look beautiful. And happier in that dress now than you were when you tried it on a few days before your wedding." Her mother crossed the room and zipped the dress up the rest of the way. She turned Alice back toward the mirror and they both looked at her in the dress. "What made you put it on today?"

"I came in here to move it to my closet—"

"Which you've been secretly doing every time someone uses this bedroom," her mother said.

Alice nodded. "So you knew."

"Of course."

"And I decided to take a peek at it."

"Does this have anything to do with working with Nate Graham at the Point?"

Alice sighed and let down her hair. "I don't regret not marrying him. But I do regret not resolving anything with him. He left for Florida right after...you know. And we haven't talked. I saw his sister once in the grocery store, but she pretended she didn't see me. That was two years ago. Nate is a big gaping hole in my past."

"And now that you work together, have you talked?"

"No. Which shouldn't surprise me, I guess. We never talked about the things that really mattered when we were engaged. At work, he pretends that nothing earth-shattering has ever happened between us. Other people at the Point don't even know we were once engaged."

"Do you plan to tell anyone?"

Alice let out a long breath. "No. It would just make people uncomfortable, as if they were tiptoeing around a sleeping giant. And it wouldn't change the fact that his feelings are still in a padded vault."

Her mother fingered the satin skirt. "Do you still love the dress?"

"It's a beautiful dress, but it's not me." Alice tried to articulate why it didn't resonate with her anymore. "It reflects my idea of what a bride looked like when I was in high school and college. What I thought a bride should look like."

"And now?"

"I've seen a lot of brides since I got involved in weddings at Starlight Point. And I think the ones who are the most beautiful are the ones who are just themselves—no puffy sleeves or cathedral trains."

Her mother stooped and pulled out the long train until it extended the length of a person behind Alice. She glanced up, smiling. "Too much?"

"Definitely."

"So what are you going to do with this?" her mother asked as she put an arm around Alice. "You can't keep schlepping it from closet to closet for the rest of your life."

Alice laughed. "That is a terrible picture you just painted." She held up her arms.

"Unzip me and get me out of this, and then we're stuffing it back in the bag. It finally occurred to me that you own a clothing resale shop, and there may be a bride out there who would be perfect for this dress."

CHAPTER SEVENTEEN

ON THE WEDNESDAY before Thanksgiving, the corporate office at Starlight Point was in holiday mode. Nate tried to work on the back-end coding for the online ticket sales system he was putting together for the next season, but the Christmas music drew him right back to the present. Holiday tunes and laughter coming from the lobby area were much more appealing than his solitary office and computer.

Nate headed to the lobby, where wide glass doors offered a view of the midway and comfortable red upholstered chairs and wood tables were scattered in groups. Usually. In honor of the holidays, the chairs and tables were pushed into a semicircle and a tall artificial tree towered over the lobby.

Alice was under the tree smoothing out a wide red and green tree skirt. She was on her hands and knees and half-concealed, but he couldn't mistake her auburn hair among the low branches.

"We have cookies and punch," Jack announced as soon as Nate appeared at the end of the hall. "We never get anything done on the day before Thanksgiving. Usually it's the way-off season, but even this year we can't be too serious."

"There's a small price for cookies," Evie said. She held up a box of Christmas lights. "Somebody—" she sent a scathing look at her brother "—didn't wind them back on the holder last year when that somebody put them away."

"I could go buy new lights," Jack offered. "So the new guy doesn't have to suffer."

"If I untangle those," Nate asked, "will I be an honorary member of the Hamilton family?"

"You already are," June put in, "by virtue of being crazy enough to work here. And willing to risk your life on the ice to promote our business."

"I'll help you," Alice offered. She stood and smoothed her hair, which had snagged on the branches.

"Thanks," Nate said, smiling. Untangling

lights with Alice would be much safer than circling the ice. He'd replayed the video Henry took of that moment when Alice had pulled him to standing and they almost kissed. Her face was turned away from the camera. How he wished he could replay her expression! His face in the video showed every vulnerability in his body, and it scared him to death.

"Employees of the year," Jack announced.

Alice laughed. "Wait until you see how successful we are."

Virginia held open the glass doors for Henry as he bumped through with a ladder. He set up the ladder next to the tall tree and headed for the table filled with food and drinks. Nate approached the food table, too. Trays overflowing with Christmas cookies sat on the red tablecloth.

"Augusta sent those," Jack said. "There is never a shortage of sweets with her around."

"You're a lucky man," Nate commented. He picked up a cookie shaped like a carousel horse and artistically decorated in red and green icing.

"No doubt," Jack said. "I loved the ice skating video you posted on our social media. I have no idea what to expect from these December weekends in terms of attendance—Evie's the one sleeping with all the spreadsheets and financials under her pillow—but it sure is fun to see this place in a different way. An ice skating rink and Christmas tree lot in the parking lot? I never thought I'd see it."

"Trees arrive next week," Alice said. She poured a small glass of red punch and raised the glass to Jack and Nate. "The tree lot will be rimmed with big old-fashioned white lights on strings, just like in the movies."

Jack walked over to greet the year-round employees who were arriving for the decorating party.

"We better get those lights on before people start trying to decorate the tree," Nate said. "We don't need any more obstacles."

Alice laughed. "Ready when you are."

June turned up the music, and the speakers she'd clearly borrowed from live shows filled the building with Christmas tunes. As more people arrived, the noise level grew and drowned out side conversations. Nate and Alice worked close together so they could hear each other, but no one else was likely to overhear their conversation.

"How are things?" Nate asked. It was less than he wanted to say, but he needed some kind of opening.

Alice found the plug end of a strand of lights and handed it to him. "Hold this while I unravel this line." She untangled and moved slowly backward. "Things are good. Weddings are planned for all the December weekends, and my mother is making mashed potatoes for Thanksgiving dinner tomorrow."

Nate leaned forward to hear her as she got farther away. "Are mashed potatoes still your favorite?"

"I could live on them," she shouted over a classic version of "Jingle Bell Rock."

"Gravy?"

She nodded. "Still haven't given it up." Alice started back toward him, looping the untangled lights around her arm as she walked.

"You haven't changed, Alice."

She worked tangles out of the lights in her hands, patiently feeding loops through other loops until they were free. She avoided looking at him. "I have changed. You just don't know me well enough to be able to tell."

Nate put his hand on hers. "After we untangle these lights and get them on the tree, will you meet me somewhere? If we're going to keep working together, we should talk." It was the riskiest thing Nate had done in years, inviting conversation—personal conversation—with the woman who'd broken his heart and driven him deeper into his shell.

Would she agree? Alice focused on untangling an especially convoluted knot before she finally looked at him. "You want to talk."

He nodded and then retreated up the ladder. He reached a hand down for the string of lights and Alice gave it to him. Knowing her penchant for the truth, even if they were in public and it could cause a scene, Nate now regretted bringing up the subject of their relationship in a crowded room filled with his employers and coworkers.

He should have stuck with his usual policy of keeping his mouth safely shut. He draped lights on the upper branches while Alice fed him the string up the ladder. He waited for one strand, moved the ladder and then placed another. The waiting was torture and he'd nearly finished the lights before she stepped up on a rung of the ladder below him so only he could hear what she had to say.

"I wanted to talk years ago," she said. "I tried to talk to you about our wedding and what should have been our marriage. But you wouldn't. Five years is a long time to wait for the other half of the conversation."

Standing high on the ladder, his head level with the top of the tree, Nate felt as if he were alone in the wilderness. He'd worked up the nerve to ask Alice what had changed her mind somewhere between the engagement ring and wedding ring, but she wasn't going to make it easy for him. He looked down at her and wondered if he would ever understand.

She climbed down and walked over to an open box of shiny ornaments.

"While you're up there," Jack yelled, "you can put on the topper. It's your reward." Jack stood below the ladder and handed up a large silver star. Nate connected it to the strand of lights, and people applauded when the star lit up, but his heart felt cold and dark.

"THANKS FOR MEETING with us on the day before Thanksgiving," Greg said. "It was one of the few times we could get together on a weekday when we weren't both working." The prospective groom finally looked up from his phone and when his fiancée frowned at him, he shoved it in his pocket.

"I could always meet you on a weekend, too," Alice said, shaking hands with both Lisa and Greg. "Starlight Point is not exactly a nine-to-five operation.

"Thanks for that. After all, it's only three weeks until our wedding," Lisa said.

Alice gestured toward the two chairs across from her desk, inviting the couple to sit. She closed her office door to block out the sounds of the Christmas tree trimming ceremony in the lobby. She had skipped lunch, instead subsisting on cookies and punch. The sugar in her bloodstream made her feel shaky.

Maybe it was her odd conversation with Nate. Why, especially during the daunting task of untangling strings of lights, did he suddenly decide he wanted to talk about their relationship? Alice suspected he was afraid people would find out and he was trying to do damage control ahead of time. That's what a good public relations man would do.

"Three weeks to live," the groom joked.

"Not funny," Lisa said. Her face colored and she turned away from Greg.

"I was just kidding. You've lost your sense of humor over this whole wedding thing," he protested.

"That's because it's serious. My parents have spent a fortune, hundreds of people are coming and you haven't done anything to help with the planning."

"I'm here now, aren't I?"

Alice leaned against her closed office door and fought the nerves fluttering in her chest. Lisa's voice rose a little higher as she continued to tick off a list of things she had to get done before their wedding, and Greg's posture became straighter and more defensive with each item. By the time she got to gifts for the groomsmen, they were both flushed and frowning.

Why did it have to be this way? This should be the happiest time of their lives.

"Let's not think about the wedding first," Alice suggested. "Tell me about your honeymoon plans." She sat in her desk chair and waited. This trick had worked before. Stressed out couples who suddenly projected themselves beyond the ceremony and on the beach instead visibly relaxed. They usually started chatting about their travel plans and spending time alone.

Not this couple. Silence.

"He's supposed to be planning that part," Lisa said quietly. "He says it's a surprise, and I got my passport renewed months ago, just in case. Lately, though, I've started to think he hasn't done anything. "

"I'm sure he has," Alice said.

Greg swallowed and put both hands on his knees as if steeling himself for battle.

"Traveling at Christmas is expensive," he said. "And flights and hotels are already booked."

"We've been planning this wedding since last Christmas," Lisa said. "Those flights and hotels weren't booked last spring. You couldn't have thought ahead?"

"I'm sorry, okay? I'm trying."

"No, you're not. If you were really trying, you'd have managed something. I'm starting to think you don't even want to marry me," the bride said.

"You know," Alice said, "we had a pre-Christmas party this morning, and I think there's plenty of cookies and punch left. I'm going to run down the hall and bring back some treats, and then we can talk about your wedding, which is going to be *just fine*."

She breezed down the hallway, took two red plates and loaded them with cookies and poured two cups of punch.

"Need help with that?" Nate asked.

"I'm going back to my office. These snacks are for the bride and groom at my meeting."

"I'll bring the punch and follow you."

Great. She appreciated his help, but having Nate right on her heels delivering punch was not conducive to facing a pre-wedding drama while remaining serene.

"I don't think that's a good idea," she said. "The meeting is…not going well. But you can come if you want."

The bride and groom were still arguing when Alice and Nate entered her office. Apparently sensing the tension, Nate delivered the punch wordlessly and slid out the door. Alice noticed he left the door open, but she didn't bother to close it. Maybe the cheerful music still wafting down the hallway would help.

The groom picked up a cookie and ate it in a single bite.

"So what are you saying?" he mumbled, still chewing. "You don't want to get married now?"

"Really?" Lisa demanded. "You think it's that simple. Yes or no, I do or don't want to get married?"

"Well, do you or don't you?"

Uh-oh. Greg did not seem to realize he was digging his hole deeper by making the issue black or white. Alice needed to ask the couple about final details, such as the exact number of guests for the caterers and if they'd finally chosen a photographer. But those questions would only be fuel on the fire, and they were possibly even moot.

A shadow passed by the door. Was Nate still out there? The pressure in Alice's chest increased. "Maybe we could talk about this another day when you're less stressed," she suggested. "Tomorrow is Thanksgiving, and holidays tend to magnify everything."

The bride and groom stared at each other. Two people who were in love—enough to plan a life together—were now reduced to squabbling in a stranger's office. Alice wanted to cry for them, but she had to maintain her composure.

"Or you could take a little walk around Starlight Point and come back refreshed," she suggested. *The cool air would help...wouldn't it?*

"It won't help," the bride said. A sob escaped her and tears gushed down her face. "He's been like this all along. It's like he doesn't even want to go through with it."

"I asked you to marry me, didn't I?" he shouted.

"A year ago," Lisa choked out. "A long year."

"Couples often spend a year planning their weddings," Alice interjected. "It takes time to get the details right." She remembered spending almost a year planning the one she'd walked out on. If only she'd stopped obsessing about the flowers, the dress and what shoes her bridesmaids should wear, she might have asked herself the hard questions she should have. Was she ready to marry Nate, even though her heart told her something was out of balance?

For months, she had believed the scale tilted far more in one direction than the other until she finally realized she couldn't marry the man she loved with all her heart because she wasn't sure the love was equally reciprocated. She loved him too much to marry him when she wasn't sure of his love.

"Which of you," Alice blurted out in a moment of reckless honesty, "loves the other one more?"

"I do," Lisa said quickly.

Greg said nothing. Lips parted, he was speechless.

Alice closed her eyes and let out the breath she'd been holding. She'd been sure he would say *I do* at the same time.

Tears flowed faster down the bride's face as she headed for the door. "Wait," Greg said, finding his voice. "Are you calling off our wedding?"

Lisa kept moving and Greg hurried after her. Alice jumped to her feet and followed the pair into the hallway.

"You can't call off the wedding three weeks before it's supposed to happen," Greg shouted. "What are we going to tell people?"

Lisa had made it to the lobby and the room full of people still enjoying the decorating party fell silent.

"That's what you're worried about? What we're going to tell people?"

"Come on. You know I love you," Greg said.

Alice waited. Maybe that was the right thing to say to get this train back on the tracks.

"How would I know that?" Lisa asked.

"Because I said so," he said. His words were choked and Alice believed he really meant them, but the situation was beyond simple words now. Greg turned to Alice. "Talk some sense into her," he said. "Tell her it's just bridal nerves or something. This is your job, right?"

Alice swallowed the lump in her throat. Everyone in the room was listening, including Nate, who had followed them and was now standing under the spreading branches of the Christmas tree.

"I'm sorry," she said. "You have to work this out for yourselves." Her nerves were at their breaking point, and she was afraid to say much.

"But you think we should get married, don't you?" the groom insisted.

Alice looked at the bride's tear-streaked face. Her agony showed in every drop that had stained the front of her blouse. The room was silent, waiting for her answer.

I'm the wedding planner. In charge of happy endings. Everyone—especially the Hamiltons, who'd taken a business risk on specialty weddings—expected her to say yes. Yes, the bride and groom should absolutely get married right before Christmas with a sleigh ride through the park and red roses and silver stars in the ballroom. Just as they had planned.

The bride kept her eyes fixed on Alice's. She had to tell her the truth. How would she live with herself if she didn't?

Alice took a deep breath and flicked a glance toward Nate. "No," she said quietly but clearly. "I don't think you should get married. Not until you've worked this through."

The bride turned and sped through the glass doors.

"Thanks a lot," the groom said bitterly. He shoved through the doors behind his fiancée.

No one in the room said anything for a moment. The entire Hamilton family with their spouses were there as well as Gloria, Henry and a handful of year-round employees.

"I can't imagine calling off your wedding only three weeks beforehand," Evie said.

"Don't you think you should have encouraged them to stick with it?"

"I…" Alice began, but she couldn't think what to say.

"At least the guy got three weeks," Nate said. "Better than finding out the night before."

Alice felt the breath leave her body and her face went numb.

"What are you talking about?" Jack asked.

Nate clammed up and his face went white. Alice could only imagine how shocked he was that he'd said something so personal in front of other people. His PR neutral smile was gone, but the damage was done.

"He's talking about me," she said. She heard someone gasp, and seeing the surprised looks on the faces of people she liked and worked with made her feel exposed and guilty. Trying on the unworn wedding dress at home had been a lot easier than revealing to Starlight Point's staff that their wedding planner was herself a runaway bride.

Nate shook his head, as if asking her not to say he was the one she'd left. She had to say it, wanted to say it. The truth, no matter how painful, was the one thing she had learned to count on. But she could only expose the part of the truth she owned. The owner of the rest of the story had to do that for himself.

"I left someone at the altar with only hours to spare," she said.

She waited for Nate to reveal that he was the one jilted. Everyone in the room could guess it, couldn't they? Why wouldn't he say it?

Nate pulled his face into his *everything's fine* smile. "I believe there's still some punch left in that bowl on the table." *How the heck did he manage to sound glib and jovial?* "We should drink a toast to whoever that poor guy was."

Several people laughed, and Alice felt her cheeks brim with humiliation as she left the party. Her passion for exposing the truth had exposed only herself.

"Hey," June called after her. Alice was halfway to her office, where she intended to grab her purse and coat and take off for the Thanksgiving holiday weekend. "You okay?"

"Fine," she said. She turned and pasted on a smile that was a complete lie. "It's water under the bridge. Happy Thanksgiving!"

It was kind of June to care about Alice's

feelings, and Alice wanted to spare her any worry. But she wished Nate had been the one to rush after her.

CHAPTER EIGHTEEN

"I DID THE MATH," Evie announced. "And I'm not just using this as an excuse. It was almost the same price for me to have a caterer prepare all this food than it would have been for me to buy it myself and prepare it. If you consider my time as a valuable commodity—which it is—it's a wash."

"So Scott can put away the fire extinguisher?" Jack asked. "I'm sure he's disappointed."

"I'm not that bad a cook. It came down to practical finance."

"And you can't argue with the results," Henry said. He helped Evie peel back the foil covers on the warming trays delivered only moments earlier by the caterer. It was so nice being invited to a family Thanksgiving after years of being in airports and cockpits. He could easily get used to being part of this family. "The food smells delicious."

"I had the caterer slice the turkey for us," Evie added.

"Come on," Henry said. "That's the best part. You get to use sharp implements and be a hero."

Henry thought he'd get a laugh, but instead Evie looked flummoxed, Jack looked out the window and Virginia looked as if she might cry. What had he said?

After a moment, conversation started back up when Scott and Caroline related a funny story about someone they knew who ordered Chinese food every year on Thanksgiving. Henry breathed again and searched for some way to either be useful or blend in. Even though his sister had invited him to her family's celebration every year, he had only gone twice because he'd volunteered to work holiday shifts. It paid well and gave him the satisfaction of helping his colleagues who had spouses and children.

He'd always suspected he was missing out, but it's hard to know what you don't know.

One by one, everyone moved down the kitchen counter and filled their plates from the catering bins. Sliced turkey, sweet potatoes, green beans, gravy, salad, rolls and assorted finger foods for the kids. Henry handed out plates, claiming he was trying to decide what to eat while he waited for everyone else, but really wanting to make himself useful.

June put a bottle of wine on the kitchen counter and dug through the drawer near Henry for a corkscrew. "That was always my father's job," she whispered. "Carving the turkey. It's been five years since he passed away, but it's still a taboo topic for some reason."

"Oh."

"You didn't know," June said. "Family holidays are minefields waiting for some poor sucker to misstep."

"Any other tips you might want to share?"

"Just be yourself." June used the corkscrew to work the cork out of the bottle of red wine. "My mother likes you for a reason."

"Do you?"

She poured two glasses. "I want her to be happy."

Another advantage of going last through the food line was scoping out exactly where he was supposed to sit. He'd already tallied up the number of people and chairs, and the numbers matched. By the time he sat down, there would only be one choice, so he couldn't screw it up. What if Ford Hamilton had always occupied the head of the table? Should he avoid sitting there?

June handed her husband, Mel, a glass of wine and sat with him and their two children. Jack, Augusta and their daughter were on the same side of the long table. Evie, Scott, Caroline and Matt were on the other side with Virginia and one empty chair—his only choice. Henry had never met Ford Hamilton, but he knew the guy had to be something special to be the head of Starlight Point and a wonderful family like this. How could he ever compete?

He couldn't. Plain and simple. All he could do was take June's advice and be himself. And take the empty seat next to Virginia.

"Next year we'll have another new family member," Augusta said.

Henry froze for a moment and then realized what she was talking about. Evie's baby.

"And I hope it won't be long before we hear good news about another one," Augusta continued.

Flying a jet with three hundred souls on board was less stressful than this.

"Don't look at me," Caroline said. "I need

a few more years of police work under my belt before Matt talks me into producing the next generation of construction engineers."

"Be a team player," Jack said. "We're going to need new rides built, and if we keep it in the family, it's a win for everyone."

"It's a holiday," Virginia said. "You'll have to take over the amusement park world after dessert."

"About that," Evie said. She swallowed and held up one hand as if she had something important to say. "I didn't get pumpkin pie this year."

"But we've always had that. It was your father's favorite," Virginia protested. Henry watched the faces of the family members, wondering if this was one of the landmines June mentioned.

Evie turned white and got up from the table. Scott jumped up and followed her as she went toward the hall leading to the bathroom.

"It's either the color or texture," he explained over his shoulder. "She's hardly had morning sickness all fall, but one look at pumpkin pie and she's...well, you know."

Virginia laughed, dispelling the tension. "There's always next year."

The talk turned to family issues involving cousins, in-laws and other extended members Henry didn't know. They discussed school and preschool, and changes they were making to their houses. The chances of local sports teams in football and the upcoming basketball seasons. All the things normal families talked about around the dinner table. Evie returned with more color in her cheeks, drank some water and ate a dinner roll.

The meal was friendly, personal, loving. June tried to include him in the conversation when it switched to travel, and Scott asked questions about airplanes. Matt wanted to know about his favorite airports and their construction and design. Henry enjoyed the food, conversation and the possibility he could belong to a family—something he deeply regretted missing out on. Was it too late for him?

Being next to Virginia stirred feelings other than regret. Spending most of the last year with her had made him realize he could spend the next year and the next. When he touched her hand or she smiled up at him to share something she already knew he understood, the emotion was as sweet as the brief kisses they had exchanged. There was already more than friendship and Henry hoped it was the tip of the iceberg.

He'd had romances and relationships over the years. A few of them stretched into months and one a little longer, but they had never given him the feeling he had now. The feeling that if it ended, he would be alone on an island, devastated. The longing he felt and the physical need to scoot his chair closer to Virginia's—this had to be love, and it was terrifying. Not because of what he felt, but because he didn't know what she felt.

"You're awfully quiet," Virginia said. She leaned close and her hair brushed his cheek. Heat radiated throughout his chest and spread up his neck and face. "Are you all right? I know it's getting a little hot in here with the fireplace going and all these people."

"I'm fine," he said.

"Well, you might want to run because the torture is about to begin. Family movies. Old ones from when the kids were little. We've been watching some every year, and this year we're up to Jack's third grade play and Evie's first steps."

Was she giving him an out in case the movies made him uncomfortable, or did she want him to leave because it was none of his business? As much as he'd come to like and even love the Hamiltons, maybe he was fooling himself if he thought they were his family.

"I planned to step out to the nursing home and visit my mother's sister."

"You still have an aunt in Bayside?"

Henry nodded. "She lived with my parents for years until her health deteriorated. I try to visit her at least once a week now that I'm her only relative in the area."

Virginia put a hand on his. "That's really nice."

Was she going to offer to go with him?

"You should make up a plate of food and take it to her. There's plenty left and it's probably better than what she's getting there."

So much for offering to go with him. Instead, she was offering him a graceful exit.

"MASHED POTATOES AND GRAVY, hold everything else," Alice's mother said as she handed her a plate.

Her sister Lauren grinned and turned to her twin four-year-old daughters. "I think this all started with a potato costume for the school play when she was in second grade."

"I was a tree that year," Mallory explained to Todd, who'd recently gone from being her boyfriend to her fiancé. "All the kindergarteners were."

"I'm glad you don't eat trees as a result," he said.

"I could be a tree hugger, though. I'm looking for a good way to use my environmental science degree."

"You should have majored in something practical like education," Lauren said. "I have a job."

"Good for you," Mallory said, raising a glass of wine to her eldest sister. "You were always the smart one."

"Hey," Alice said. "I thought I was the smart one. At least I save all my calories for foods I truly love instead of worrying about balancing out my plate."

Alice's mother stood at the head of the table and pointed her serving spoon and fork at her three daughters. "I've missed you, bickering and all."

The mashed potatoes were amazing. Made from scratch with heavy whipping cream and plenty of butter. Even when Alice was thirteen and worried about how she looked in her skimpy figure skating outfits, she'd never departed from her love affair with her favorite food.

It had been on the menu for her wedding— rehearsal dinner and reception. She always advised brides to consider the dietary expectations of their guests for most of the food selections, but she also encouraged them to include the one thing they considered comfort food. For some brides, it was chocolate, for others buttery biscuits and for one notable bride it had been caviar. Comfort comes in all price ranges.

"So how's the wedding business at the Point?" Lauren asked. "I would have gotten married there if they were doing weddings a few years ago."

"They started booking fast this past season, and next year looks solid already," Alice said.

"How'd you get started planning weddings?" Todd asked.

"I started off doing special events like

beautiful baby contests and sand castle parties on the beach, but then the Hamiltons shifted me over to weddings because that's where the money is. I'm now in charge of colors, flowers, cakes, pictures, invitations and every other wedding decision the bride wants help with."

"That sounds hard," Todd said. He put down his fork and turned to Mallory. "Are you sure you want to marry me if you have to face all those choices?"

"We have an expert in the family," she said and stood up. "What do you think about a June wedding for us next year?"

It wasn't just a question. It was also an announcement. Mallory and Todd had been vaguely engaged with no definite date for at least a year.

Their mother put down her serving implements and smiled broadly at her youngest daughter. "Have you finally picked a date? Can I get my dress now that I know what season and century the wedding will be in?"

Mallory grinned. "We're thinking second weekend in June, but we're going to need professional help."

"Here in Bayside?" Alice asked. She was

already scrolling through possible venues on her phone. June was a tricky choice because of its popularity. Would anything be available only seven months out?

"I was thinking maybe at Starlight Point," her sister said. "We looked at all the wedding information on the website and started falling in love with the idea. That's when I also noticed *someone's* name listed as the PR man for the Point."

"You mean Nate Graham," Alice's father said reasonably, as if he wasn't dropping a grenade into the family conversation.

Alice nodded. "We work together."

"How?" Lauren asked. "Isn't it awkward?"

"The same way you work with anyone. I'm sure you don't love every single one of your seventh graders and their parents, but you find common ground, right?" she asked Lauren.

"With almost all of them. But some of them, sheesh, I'm just hoping they grow up over Thanksgiving break. Or move to a different school district."

"It must be weird seeing Nate all the time," Mallory added. "You're braver than I am."

Her sisters didn't mean harm. They'd been

there for her after the wedding and cheerfully sacrificed the cash they'd spent on matching dresses and shoes. They probably really did think Alice was fine…even brave.

But they didn't know about the previous day's humiliation at Starlight Point when Nate had refused to acknowledge being a party to her failed wedding. He'd left her dangling in front of the whole room as if she were a broken bulb on a Christmas tree. It hurt her more than she wanted to admit.

But her sisters clearly believed her to be over it. Her mother had probably even told them that the unused wedding gown was on sale at her shop. *Over it.*

"Well," Alice said lightly. "Starlight Point is a big place. It's not that hard to ignore Nate Graham and focus instead on the most perfect day in the life of *other* brides."

Her mother finally sat down now that all the plates were filled. "Do you ever wonder what happens to those couples after they get married?" she asked.

"I hope they go on an awesome honeymoon someplace where there are no children," Lauren said, sighing as she spoke. "I could use one of those about now."

"I'd like to imagine the bride and groom looking just as happy as they did during their first dance all the rest of their lives," Alice said.

Her father laughed and everyone turned toward him. "What? Based on my personal experience, I think Alice has the right idea."

Her mother leaned over and kissed her dad. "I was already planning to cut your slice of apple pie bigger than all the other ones, but now I'm giving you two slices."

CHAPTER NINETEEN

ON FRIDAY EVENING, Starlight Point sparkled with shimmering snowflakes and miles of red ribbon. Even Alice traded in her favorite pink clothing for Christmas red—deep red that wouldn't clash with her auburn hair. She wanted to be everywhere at once, just to gauge the reception of her plans and the excitement.

"It's incredible," June breathed, her eyes alight with the holiday spirit. She stood next to Alice between the ice rink and the Christmas tree lot. Where hundreds of cars usually sweltered in summer heat, ice skaters and evergreens took a place on the asphalt. "Even better than I expected. When I saw all these plans last February, I was definitely impressed. But with snow and people and music everywhere…we've just got to do this every year. Maybe even bigger next year."

"Whoa," Alice said. "Let's see how the attendance figures tally up or your sister won't approve five dimes for next year."

"Oh," June said, waving her hand in the air. "Evie will be distracted by her new baby. It'll loosen her up. Having a family does that to you—makes you put things in perspective."

Alice nodded. She didn't doubt June's words a bit, but she wondered if she would ever have a chance to find out for herself.

At one time, she'd thought she had her entire life planned out. Did she regret not marrying Nate back then? No. But if she could go back in time and force him to face the truth, she would do it. And what was the truth? Had her perspective been off, shoved sideways by her own youth and the stress of planning a wedding? Did he really not love her enough to open his heart? She had recently begun to think she'd misjudged him because of the glimpses of emotion she'd noticed. But after the scene at the office party, she had no doubt she'd been right about him.

"I'm dying to see my mother dressed as Mrs. Claus. And we were very lucky to get Henry to volunteer for the big part. Apparently he's never heard the horror stories of department store Santas being tortured by children."

"He'll be good-humored about it," Alice said. "He may be the nicest man I know."

"Hard to believe no woman has ever snatched him up," June said. "But then again, I know of several perfectly lovely people who are obstinately single."

Alice cleared her throat.

"That was me for a while until I got over it," June continued.

Alice wondered what June's thoughts were on her mother and Henry, but it wasn't her place to ask. No matter how much she wanted to.

"Tonight Santa and Mrs. Claus are greeting children at the front gate, but tomorrow there's a dramatic arrival via icebreaker boat in the marina," Alice said. "I hope I didn't go too big on that one."

"Can't go too big. This is Starlight Point. And it's Christmas."

June headed for the front gates, and Alice wandered through the trees for sale in the cheerfully lit tree lot. Would anyone come to Starlight Point to buy the family Christmas tree? She hoped so. Even if they didn't, the scent of evergreens among the snow set the scene for guests' entrance into the amusement park, where they'd find a holiday wonderland. Only a selection of rides were open, but the midway invited guests to stroll beneath the lights.

As she walked among the trees, trailing her fingers along the branches of one tree and then the next, she passed little kids dressed in colorful winter coats and hats. Their parents also wore festive winter clothes. Alice loved winter in Michigan and, like everyone else, had learned to tolerate the cold and even enjoy it. Would Nate gain his winter tolerance back if he stuck around? Was he planning to stay? Judging him based upon his work performance, Alice believed he loved his job at Starlight Point.

But she also knew that wasn't the real reason he had come home.

As Alice approached the checkout area, she saw Nate at the cash register. He had a small evergreen wreath looped over his arm. Was it for his office or his front porch? She paused, wondering if it was too late to avoid him. The sting of her last encounter with him was still painful. She had talked with June and

Evie, and they had surprised her by not being upset about her role in the recently canceled wedding, which had been scheduled for right before Christmas. They'd had some pointed questions about her and Nate, but Alice had declined answering them. It was only half her story to tell, and she doubted that Nate's guard would ever slip far enough for him to talk about it.

Nate turned and stopped when he saw her. He wore the red hat and scarf from her office and he noticed her looking at them. "Sorry I never returned these," he said. "Can you believe I haven't bought my own?"

"Keep them as long as you like. I have extras." Alice did not stop to chat, preferring instead to continue with her plan of taking a loop through Starlight Point to see the holiday decorations. Thanksgiving break had been over for a week, her sisters had gone home and three different women had tried on the wedding dress displayed prominently in her mother's shop. Alice was ready to enjoy the spirit of the holidays without baggage—and that included Nate.

"I owe you an apology. And a thank you," he said. He caught her arm as she passed him.

"Maybe one of those," she said.

"I shouldn't have made that comment about three weeks' notice."

Alice crossed her arms as an excuse for pulling away from Nate. "It didn't help the situation."

"But you…let me take the coward's way out by not revealing I was the man you—"

"Jilted on the eve of our wedding," she said. "Fine. Apology accepted. I need to get going."

Nate swept a glance around. The evergreens in rows combined with loud Christmas music gave them a private space to talk. Did he intend to talk? Now?

"Why didn't you marry me?"

If Santa's sleigh led by reindeer had careened past, Alice couldn't have been more surprised. Wasn't she the one who asked tough questions?

"I told you at the time," Alice said. Her throat was thick. The holiday music was reminiscent of her childhood and she heard laughter from the park.

"You said you were too young, that you weren't ready."

Alice didn't answer. The music changed to a cheerful holiday tune about being jolly.

"I never believed that was your real reason," Nate said. "We were the same age."

"And?"

A family of four walked past. The father and the older daughter carried a tree while the younger daughter held a candy cane in one hand and her mother's hand in the other.

Nate waited until they were well beyond earshot. "I wasn't too young."

"Not everyone is the same," Alice said. Although she'd faced her own feelings long ago and come to terms with the truth about their relationship, she didn't see the point in rehashing the past with Nate. Why would he understand now, and what difference would it make?

"Why are you bringing this up now?" she asked.

Nate took off the red cap and ran his hand through his hair. "It was nice going away. Living in another state made it easier to forget… things. And people. But coming home…" He put the hat back on and adjusted the wreath on his arm. "Coming home has reminded me that there are people who will always be in my heart. No matter how hard it was to say goodbye to them."

Alice realized in a horrible stab of guilt and sorrow what the wreath was for. His mother's grave. They had almost never talked about his mother's sudden death when he was twelve. Raw sorrow showed on his face for a moment, and the unexpected sight shocked Alice into wanting to pull him close and hug away every bad thing that had happened to him. Except she was one of those bad things, and he wouldn't let her close enough to help erase the damage.

"Did you love me?" Nate asked.

"With all my heart. And that was the problem," Alice said. She brushed past Nate and stumbled through the row of closely stacked pine trees, trying to put more than five years of distance between herself and the man who had broken her heart.

CHAPTER TWENTY

NATE WANTED TO relax and enjoy the day at Starlight Point. Aside from taking a few pictures and some mental notes for a blog entry on the amusement park's website, he wasn't really on the clock. He was there to make sure his dad got out of the house and his nephew had a good time. Even though Nate had purposely not included video of himself on the ice with Alice, his dad and sister knew he'd attempted to skate that day and he was the great family hope on the ice now.

"Uncle Nate," his nephew said as he waited next to him on the bench, "can you tie this?"

"Sure." Nate bent to help the five-year-old who looked like a miniature version of his grandfather.

"If you've got Cody," his sister commented, "Dad and I might find someplace warmer to pass the time."

Nate nodded. "I recommend the coffee

shop right inside the front gate. You can stay warm and still watch the carousel and the people."

"Not a bad idea."

Nate leaned over to tie his own rented skates and saw a flash of red go past. He turned his head and discovered Alice moving swiftly among the skaters already there early on a Saturday morning. She could outpace him on the ice easily despite his clumsy efforts to keep up. There was no keeping up with Alice, not with a woman who seemed to have no fear.

She had walked away—run away—yesterday night when they'd gotten dangerously close to wading into the past. What on earth had she meant by what she said? Who loves a person with all her heart and then refuses to marry him?

As he'd driven home, he'd thought about how lucky he was that Alice had run off through the pine trees and refused to get in deep. Did she have any idea how close he'd come to breaking down and telling her how deeply he'd been hurt by her rejection and how many nights he'd spent thinking of her over the past five years?

Those were obviously thoughts best left unspoken.

Nate took his nephew's hand and guided him to the edge of the ice. "Ready, big guy? I'm no professional, but I've skated one more time than you have so I can give you a few pointers."

"Ready."

Nate kept one hand on the railing and held his nephew's hand with the other. They took tentative steps with Nate struggling to hold them both up. He tried to remember Alice's advice.

"Bend your knees a little," he said. "Put your weight in your thighs and keep your back straight."

Just as he offered this advice to Cody, Alice skated past. She glanced back and smiled, but she didn't stop. He looked up at the roller coasters towering over Starlight Point. They reminded him of the emotional turmoil he and Alice were putting themselves through. But even those wild rides came to a safe stop.

Was there a happy ending for him and Alice? The thought nearly took him down to his knees. For years, he'd kept his emotions behind doors with rusted hinges and frozen locks. But now his defenses were melting. He knew what would happen. He'd been through it once before and he didn't think he could survive it again. His emotions were a constant threat to his survival. Exhaustion and worry about his father, being back in his childhood home, working daily with the woman he'd loved and lost.

No wonder the doors were creaking open. He had to keep it together for his family's sake. And his own.

Nate let go of the railing, determined to find his footing on the ice. His nephew wobbled with the sudden increase of speed, and Nate was afraid they were both going down. He didn't care about his own knees and elbows, but he had no right to endanger an innocent child. Luckily, Alice sped up on the other side of his nephew and took Cody's hand, steadying them all. She smiled at Nate.

"Hello," he said, using his rehearsed smile and a casual tone. "You saved us from a fall."

His nephew looked curiously at Alice, who was a stranger to him. A stranger! The woman who was very nearly Cody's aunt—if things had turned out differently. "This is a friend of mine," Nate said. He hesitated, unsure how much to say. Had his sister ever told Cody his uncle had been humiliated in love?

That was not the kind of thing a person told a child who wasn't even in kindergarten yet. He was being ridiculous.

"Her name is Alice Birmingham and I've known her for a long, long time," Nate told his nephew. "She's also a champion skater, so we're really lucky she came along."

"I'm not a champion," she said, laughing. "But I do love to skate, and I think you're off to a terrific start. Give you a few more laps and I'll be struggling to keep up."

Cody laughed and took a few experimental strides now that he had an adult holding both his hands. They circled the rink at an excruciatingly slow pace once, and then twice more at a more confident speed.

"You're doing great," Nate told his nephew. "Want to let go and try it on your own?"

"Okay."

The boy released both their hands and struck out on his own. By virtue of being closer to the ice and having the confidence of youth, he did better than his uncle. Nate took a different kind of risk by grabbing Alice's arm as he wobbled.

"Sorry," he said. "Remember, I'm new at this."

The boy skated out in front of them.

"About last night," he began, hoping the music and the ambient noise from the other skaters would drown out what he wanted to say.

She looked up and her cheeks were pink. Was it just the cold air?

"I've been thinking a lot—"

Nate glanced at the side of the rink and froze. His dad and sister stood at the rail watching them skate. His sister was using her phone to take pictures. What had his face revealed just a moment ago? His sister undoubtedly recognized Alice and she'd ask him tough questions later. Along with the questions would come advice. *Don't get anywhere near a woman who hurt you once.*

He focused on the ice in front of him, where his nephew wobbled bravely. He was better off keeping his promise to his sister.

"I should catch up to Cody," he said. He left without waiting for Alice's reaction, afraid he might lose his nerve and take another fall.

ALICE LEFT THE ice and walked toward the marina to catch the official arrival of Santa and Mrs. Claus on an icebreaker. *Breaking the ice.* Something she and Nate had done when they first met in August after years of silence. But the silences were still there.

She saw him standing with his family on the dock where the ship would tie up. Of course. He knew the plans, and he'd wisely maneuvered his nephew close to the action. Alice would have done the same if she were there with her own nieces and nephew. She should ask her sister to come for a long weekend so the kids could enjoy Starlight Point at Christmas. She wouldn't even have to haul the wedding gown out of the guest room closet this time.

A ship's horn sounding over and over interrupted her thoughts. The group surged toward the edge of the dock, which was, thank goodness, carefully fenced for the event. Alice stood on her tiptoes to see over the crowd. A small icebreaker usually used for keeping the shipping channels open as late into the winter as possible shoved aside the thin layer of ice in the marina. The ice crackled loudly and split into jagged pieces. Santa and Mrs. Claus in their red costumes stood at the bow, waving and smiling.

Alice got into the spirit and waved back along with all the children. As the boat got closer, Alice noticed Virginia and Henry holding hands. For balance, right? The boat docked, and before Santa disembarked, he turned to Mrs. Claus and gave her a kiss on the lips. The children squealed and laughed. Virginia put her hand over her heart and waggled a finger at Henry. Was her blush stage makeup or the real thing?

The boat bumped the dock and Virginia staggered. Chunks of ice floated in the marina and a fall from the boat would be disastrous. An audible gasp escaped the crowd. Nate jumped the fence, propped his foot on the bow and put a steadying hand on Virginia. She flailed her arms and teetered a moment, but she recovered her balance. Alice breathed. *It was going to be okay.*

Unfortunately, it wasn't over. Virginia's struggling had knocked her rescuer off balance. He stepped back and his foot missed the edge of the dock. With a horrific splash, Nate slid into the icy marina between the boat and the dock. The crowd gasped again and Alice heard at least one scream.

Without thinking twice, she raced to the edge of the dock, climbed over the fence and knelt, sweeping her arm over the edge to grab any part of Nate she could find. She knew he was a novice ice skater, but could he swim? The water soaking her sleeve was freezing. Heart pounding, she flattened herself on the dock to get a better reach. Another man next to her was doing the same thing. She grabbed something solid and pulled—the red scarf. Nate bobbed up alongside it, a look of shock on his face.

The man next to Alice grabbed Nate's coat and hauled him over the edge of the dock. Alice helped by grabbing his feet and swinging them onto the dock. The man pulled down his own scarf and hugged Nate, and Alice realized with a shock that her co-rescuer was Nate's father. Of course he'd come to help Nate. He loved him. She had also raced to the edge of the dock and ruined her leather gloves without a moment's thought. Did she love Nate, too?

"Son," Nate's father said, emotion and tension in his voice. "Are you all right?"

Nate shivered and smiled. "Freezing but fine." He sat up and waved to the crowd with a reassuring smile. Ever the showman, Alice thought, he didn't want to ruin the arrival of Santa for all the kids watching in open-mouthed wonder. But it wasn't just show… he had stepped up to save Virginia before anyone else even processed what was going on. Alice had no doubt he'd do the same for anyone. But he hadn't done it for her when she was humiliated just weeks ago.

"Ho, ho, ho," Henry called in his Santa voice. "I always like to deliver surprises at Christmas, but that was a doozy."

When the attention of the bystanders was diverted, Nate asked his father if he was okay. Father and son were both deathly pale.

"I can't believe you could haul me out of the water after all you're going through," Nate told his father. Alice couldn't believe it either. It was a testament to the power of love.

Nate's sister shoved through the crowd and took control of the situation. "You're both going home right now and getting in front of the fireplace," Nate's sister commanded. She cut a glance at Alice and almost smiled.

"Thank you," she said. She hauled her dad

and her brother to their feet and looped an arm around both of them. "Come on, Cody."

"I thought my heart was going to explode," June said as she came up beside Alice.

"Me, too, but it turned out okay."

"Are you nuts? My mother kissed a man right in front of everyone and then practically fell off the boat." June put a hand over her eyes. "I love drama, but that was over the top even by my standards."

Alice laughed, hoping to dissipate her nervous energy.

"I didn't know you were such a brave rescuer. My brother-in-law Scott would have been impressed."

"Instinct," Alice said. "I fell through the ice on the lake when I was trying to skate at my friend's tenth birthday party. Her dad pulled me out, but I remember the cold and the fear."

June smiled but didn't say anything.

"And Nate is a good PR director," Alice said as she pulled off her ruined suede gloves. "I didn't want you guys to have to replace him."

June waved to her mother and returned her attention to Alice. "I'm not sure what to think of my mother's slightly goofy level of happiness lately. Playing Mrs. Claus is no surprise. She loves children and often shows up in some wacky costume to read to the kids in the Starlight Point daycare. It's something else."

"Perhaps her...friendship...with Henry?" Alice suggested. "If I were to make a recommendation—"

June sighed. "Let's hear it."

"I'd tell you to let them figure it out. As much as I wish everything would turn out exactly as I think it should, people have to decide for themselves."

"And yet you plan weddings for people who might be making mistakes."

Alice let out a long breath. "Even though it doesn't always go how I plan, I want happy endings for everyone."

"Says the woman who just rescued her ex-fiancé from drowning," June said.

Alice didn't deny the fact as she watched Nate walk away with his family.

"For what it's worth," June continued. "I think second chances are even sweeter than the first time around."

Alice waved goodbye to June, not trusting

her voice. She stuffed her gloves in a trash-can, squared her shoulders and headed toward her office to prepare for the afternoon wedding scheduled at Starlight Point. At least she could help someone else get their happy ending.

CHAPTER TWENTY-ONE

VIRGINIA PUT STAMPS on three dozen envelopes. That was the easy part. She stuck return labels on next. She remembered the first Christmas after Ford died, when she'd used up all their old labels with both their names on them. Ordering new ones with only her name had taken her months. And now she'd grown used to seeing only *Virginia Hamilton* on the stickers.

She flipped open her address book and started writing the names of her lifetime of friends and family on the green envelopes. That was a chore, but signing her own name and not including Ford's had been the hardest part the past few years.

She wore her favorite soft yoga pants and turtleneck and settled in with a cup of coffee, determined to get the job done as quickly as possible. Letting it hang over her head was worse than the actual task, and if she didn't get these Christmas cards in the mail in the next few days, the ones traveling the farthest wouldn't make it in time for the holiday.

Gladys barked and nosed aside the curtain in the front window. It wasn't a warning bark, it was more of an excited sound. One of the kids? Virginia looked through the window and then opened the door.

"I haven't spent a whole winter back here in Michigan," Henry said, "but I do know days as nice as this in the middle of December are an early Christmas gift."

He wore a long-sleeved shirt but no coat. Warm air circulated through the door and sunshine sparkled off the lake behind him. His vintage truck sat in her driveway, its windshield reflecting the morning sun. She had been so focused on her task that she hadn't even noticed what a beautiful day it was.

"What are you up to on such a nice day?" Virginia asked, waving him into the house and closing the door behind him. He brought with him the scent of the lake and fresh air. Just what she needed.

"Anything outside."

"Coffee first?"

"Sure," he said. Henry followed Virginia into the kitchen and got two mugs from the cabinet over the stove without having to ask where she kept them.

"You got your truck painted." Virginia poured coffee into both mugs, leaving him an inch at the top for the milk she knew he'd add.

"I'm out for a ride, making sure the paint sticks before I pay the final bill."

Virginia laughed. "Is that why you ended up here?"

Henry shook his head. "I was headed here. I need someone to have fun with today. I already put up my Christmas lights yesterday and mailed cards to the same people I've been sending them to all my life."

"That's what I was doing this morning." She gestured to the end of the kitchen table, where envelopes and cards were stacked.

"I could mail those for you when I go to the post office later."

She shook her head. "I'm nowhere near ready."

"Can I convince you to put it off for the morning? I've got the itch to leave the earth for a while."

Virginia's breath caught. Henry laughed and put his hand on her shoulder.

"I mean take my plane up."

"Oh. And you want someone to go with you?"

His hand slid down her arm and his fingers laced with hers. "I want you to go with me."

She hesitated. They'd spent a lot of time together, but Henry seemed different, deliberate today. He was in her space, at her table, drinking her coffee and dragging her away from a yearly obligation. Was he challenging the status quo of their relationship?

"You're not afraid of flying, are you?" he asked.

"No, but I haven't flown in years," she said. She sipped her coffee. When was the last time? Ford had been with her. They'd flown to California, rented a car and toured the wine country and Napa Valley. She remembered a long, carefree drive down the Pacific coast. Their kids were grown up and they felt they had the rest of their lives in front of them. It seemed like another lifetime.

"It's been much too long, then," Henry

said. He rubbed the backs of her fingers as he spoke.

Her last flight had been during the *before* period of her life. Virginia had slowly realized over the past few months that she'd created a dividing line in her life when Ford died. There were the *before* and *since* eras. Maybe it was time to create a *now* and *tomorrow* era.

"You're right," she said.

"The airfield where I keep my plane is only twenty minutes away. For an added bonus, you get to ride in my pickup. The guy at the body shop called it an antique, so I had to remind him it's younger than I am. He didn't know what to say after that."

Virginia laughed. "Before we go, I think I should ask how old your plane is."

Henry kissed her cheek. "It's only two years old." He paused, his lips hovering just over hers. "Thanks for taking a chance on me."

Virginia kissed him on the lips and ran her fingers through his neatly cut hair. They had kissed before, but it was the first she'd initiated. He made her feel young and light, desirable. How much stronger would that feeling be when they were up in the air?

"You're a professional pilot," she said lightly, breaking the kiss. "So I don't get many points for bravery."

"I wasn't just talking about flying," he said.

She bit her lip. "I know."

They drove to the airport in Henry's pickup. In the narrow old-fashioned cab with a giant windshield, the sun washed over them as Henry deftly shifted gears.

"Can you drive or fly anything?" Virginia asked.

"Anything I've tried, but there are a lot of things I haven't had the chance to operate. Like helicopters, tanks, fire trucks and trains. I wouldn't mind driving a train."

"We have one at Starlight Point. I could probably make that happen."

Henry shrugged. "I wouldn't want people to say I'm using our relationship to get access to the locomotive."

What was their relationship? Virginia couldn't give it a name, but she would willingly trust Henry with her car, lawnmower or train. And her heart? That's what frightened her.

Virginia's phone dinged in her purse and she pulled it out and read a text from June.

Want me to pick you up for lunch?

Thanks, honey, Virginia answered. But I have plans.

She didn't tell her daughter what those plans were.

June responded after only seconds. I'll call u later. Love you.

Virginia dropped the phone back into her purse and turned to Henry. "Do you really own your own plane?"

"Part owner. It's pretty expensive, so I made a deal with another guy at the airport and we share it. We split the purchase price and the maintenance, and we work out the rest. I called him this morning and he's not planning to go up this week. He still works part time and his company has a project they're finishing up before the holidays."

"So it's all ours," Virginia said.

Henry slanted a glance her way. "It is."

Twenty minutes later, after a preflight check and other formalities, Virginia and Henry raced down the small airstrip and took off. Her heart lifted and adrenaline poured through her as she left the ground.

"You're smiling," Henry said. "Good sign."

"I feel like a baby bird getting out of the nest."

"Where do you want to go?"

"Oh," Virginia said. "Didn't you tell that man at the airport where we were going?"

"I filed a flight plan, but I can radio in a change. You tell me where you'd like to go."

Virginia's phone dinged and she glanced at the text from Evie.

Are you doing okay?

Fine, Virginia answered. Hope you are, too.

"Just Evie saying hello," she said as she looked out her window. Lake Huron stretched across the horizon, and they seemed to be following the shoreline. "Can we fly over Bayside and Starlight Point?"

"Sure. You've probably done that before, right?"

She shook her head. "Never. I've never been in a small plane and flown low enough to see anything familiar."

"You're about to, and I won't even have to change my flight plan. I'll try to make sure you don't miss a thing."

Henry piloted the aircraft along the shore and Virginia recognized several landmarks as they approached Bayside. She saw the beach and pier of the state park, and the downtown docks stretching into the bay.

"I never realized that the bay looks like a big teapot from the air," she said. She couldn't stop looking at something that was so familiar yet so new. Finally, she raised her eyes to the peninsula across the bay.

"Ready for a flyover of Starlight Point?"

She nodded. Her heart fluttered with excitement and nerves. She should be home addressing Christmas cards, but she was up in the air with a man who made her forget her boundaries. If she abandoned the role of wife and mother she'd always played, what would she be?

She could already see the Starlight Point peninsula jutting into the lake. Roller coasters looked two-dimensional from the air. The marina scooped a semicircle from the bay side. The white concrete midway shone in the morning sun, and the hotel's green roof spread along the beach side. The familiar midway and rides looked so different from the air. Had she never imagined what they would look like from above? What else had she been missing all these years?

"I wish my kids could see this," she said. "If I called them and told them to look up in the sky, they'd never believe what I'm doing."

"Why not?"

"Because…" Virginia couldn't think of a single reason why not. Her kids weren't the ones confining her to the role of grieving widow. She leaned closer to her window and peered down at a place she knew by heart. She would always be Ford Hamilton's wife, married in her heart to him and Starlight Point. Always be the mother to the three wonderful children who now steered the amusement park with great care and success.

But she could be herself and also welcome another love into her life. It wouldn't change the past, but it would make the future even sweeter.

"Are you having fun?" Henry asked.

"To say the least," she marveled, turning

her attention back to him. "I feel as if I'm opening my eyes for the first time."

Her phone signaled a text again and she glanced at the message from Jack. She didn't want to miss the view from the plane's window.

I dropped off some special pastries from Augusta a few minutes ago at your house, but you weren't home. I only let Gladys eat one and I put them out of reach. Love you.

"Kids again," Virginia said.

"You have great kids. And it's nice they all text you every morning."

"They don't usually."

"Is it a special occasion?" Henry asked. "Don't tell me it's your birthday and I didn't get you a card."

Virginia laughed. "My birthday's in June." She returned to her study of Starlight Point from the air, but the memory hit her a second later. It was Ford's birthday. How could she possibly have forgotten the date?

She approached it with a hole in her heart every year, but she'd been so busy with the

Christmas activities this year, she'd only given it a brief thought earlier in the week.

Her children were worried about her and missing their father, and she was flying high with another man. She had to figure out her own emotions before she hurt the people she loved.

CHAPTER TWENTY-TWO

"I CAN'T BELIEVE you called our uncle the last time this happened," Nate's sister, Susan, said. They stood just outside the emergency room doors while they waited for hospital staff to find their father a room. "He's about as comforting as a brick pillow."

"He's helpful in a crisis," Nate protested.

"For what? Telling you to dry your tears and pull yourself up by your bootstraps? Good thing he never had any kids of his own," Susan said.

Nate felt guilty for calling his sister at three in the morning, but last time he hadn't called her and she was furious. Neither of them had gotten any sleep. "You need coffee or bourbon or something," he said.

"I'm serious. Do you know what he told me at our mother's funeral? Our mother's funeral," she reiterated. "I was fifteen, bawling my eyes out, and he said I should be grateful I still had one parent left."

Nate swallowed his emotions. Being outside the emergency room doors brought back a swarm of nausea he battled with all his might.

"He also told me I should be stoic for you," Susan continued. "What the hell does that mean? You didn't need someone to be stoic. You were twelve. You needed someone to hug you and say she loves you. And that's exactly what I did."

"I remember," Nate whispered. His voice wouldn't work. His head felt hot. Maybe he had the same fever his father did, an illness that had landed him in the hospital between chemotherapy appointments again.

"Will you be all right here?" his sister asked. "I'm going to run back to Dad's house and grab a few things for him since it looks like he'll be staying at least a day or two. He asked me to bring his robe and slippers and some other stuff."

"I'll be fine. I'll text you the room number when they move him."

Nate waited outside the emergency entrance for a few more minutes. He hated walking through those doors. Years ago, he'd come here thinking he'd arrived just in time, but his mother was already gone. He stood between the two sets of doors—those leading out to the parking lot and the ones leading to his dad, waiting on a stretcher. The wide outer doors let in the relentless December cold. After a few minutes, the chill drove him inside to wait with other family members until his father got admitted to a room upstairs.

The wait gave him time to think about all the things he'd been avoiding. His mother's funeral was horrible enough, but seeing his picture in the local newspaper in an article vilifying the drunk driver was worse. His seventh-grade teacher hadn't meant for him to see it. The paper happened to be lying on her desk when he'd finally gone back to school after a week at home. How many of his classmates had seen his shocked and tearstained face, naked emotion and vulnerability all over it?

That's where he'd learned to put on a brave face. A smile that masked his inner life that was no one's business but his own. He'd pitied his father for crying alone in his room and shunned the pity his friends, their parents, his pastor, teachers, everyone had tried to give him. And Alice? She'd grown up in Bayside, and she knew what happened to his mother. They never talked about it. Had she ever seen that picture?

Finally, an hour later, Nate sat by his dad's bedside in a private room on the third floor of the hospital. He hoped his sister would get there soon with some comfort items for his dad, because he needed all the comfort he could get. They all did.

"She hasn't changed," his father said. He sat up in bed and turned bright eyes on his son.

"Susan? Nope, bossy as ever," Nate agreed. "But that's a good thing sometimes."

"Not Susan. Alice. You haven't wanted to talk about her all fall, but I know you see her every day. I thought maybe she was giving you the cold shoulder since you never mentioned her, but when you fell in the marina, she and I were the first ones there to pull you out."

Nate nodded.

"All those other bystanders hanging around, and she flew out of nowhere and started grabbing anything she could find in that water as if she'd lost a treasure in there," his father continued.

Nate remembered a hand grabbing him. Was it Alice's or his father's? When he'd bobbed to the surface in the shockingly cold water, the first face he saw was Alice's. Her face had been tortured, frightened. His father's expression was the same. Nate had tried to quickly de-escalate the situation and save face by smiling and claiming everything was just fine. And it was. With no actual harm done, he'd gone home and dried off. But his father was right about Alice. Nate had no doubt she would have dove into the water to find him if he hadn't come up quickly.

The thought brought a lump to his throat.

"I'm going to see if the nurses will bring you some breakfast," Nate said. "And I think it's a little too hot in here. I'll check on that."

"Sit down, son. Why are you so afraid to talk about this?"

"I'm not afraid, I'm just concerned for your well-being."

"I can't count how many times I've asked you if you were okay in the years since we lost your mother. Every single time you said you were fine, and every single time I didn't believe you."

"I was fine," Nate said. "Still am."

"How long do you think you can keep your outer shell in place before you admit you need other people and you're not fine? Having cancer has taught me that lesson, and it's a cruel teacher I wouldn't wish on my worst enemy, let alone my only son."

Nate went to the door and asked the nurse for a breakfast tray. When he returned to his chair by his father's bed, he thought his dad had drifted off to sleep.

"Talk to me, son," his dad said. "What are you going to do when I'm through with cancer, however it turns out?"

"I have a great job at the Point."

"Does it make you happy?"

"It's what I went to college for, and they treat me well."

"That's not what I asked. And what about Alice? What are you going to do about her?"

This was going too far. The last thing Nate wanted to do was hurt his father's feelings, especially when he was sick, but he couldn't maintain his outward calm while someone was digging around in his heart with a soup spoon.

"We're not at a slumber party, Dad. I didn't come prepared to talk about my feelings." His tone was atrocious. Talking to his father like that, especially when he was in the hospital battling cancer, was out of character. Where was his smooth PR facade he'd so carefully cultivated?

The nurse came in and checked his father's IV. She smiled at Nate and asked if he wanted some water or some coffee. He tried to flash his *everything's fine* smile, but it wouldn't work. The nurse told him she was bringing him coffee even though he hadn't asked. Even a stranger could tell he wasn't okay.

"Why are you so afraid?" his father asked after the nurse left.

Nate thought he was going to lose it. He'd listened to his father sobbing in his room at night. Had his father also listened outside his door, wondering when he was going to cry?

"Well," Nate said, "my mother was killed by a drunk driver when I was twelve and my fiancée dumped me at the altar ten years later. So you can imagine how much I *don't* love talking about my feelings."

"What the hell is wrong with you?" Susan asked. She'd come into the room at the absolute wrong moment.

Nate put his head in his hands with the intention of avoiding the looks his father and sister were giving him. Instead, to his utter horror, he started to cry. He shook with sobs until he couldn't breathe. His father swung out of bed to put an arm around him, and his sister patted his back and told him she loved him.

He hadn't been so ashamed of himself since his mother's funeral.

VIRGINIA SUMMONED HER courage and knocked on Henry's front door. Although just past seven, the evening was completely dark except for the brightly colored Christmas bulbs wrapped around the porch posts and strung through the bushes.

Was she making a big mistake? What if Henry didn't feel the same way about her that she felt about him? There was only one way to find out, and she hadn't survived fifty-seven years on the planet by being a coward.

Henry opened the porch door. His eyebrows went up and his smile went wide. "Virginia! Come in!"

She stepped into the rectangle of light and warmth and Henry pulled the door shut. *Very promising so far.* He had not asked her what she was doing there. If he had, her plan was to say her car was making a funny noise and she was in the neighborhood. She hadn't believed she would need that flimsy excuse, but she was new to the business of putting her heart in risky situations.

"I know I was taking a chance," she said. "That you'd be home, I mean."

Henry spread his arms wide. "Here I am." Without ceremony, he pulled her close and kissed her. "You've never been to my house," he said. "I'm so glad you came."

"I was afraid I might be intruding."

He laughed. "You've been in my airplane and your dog knows which of my pockets to find treats in. We have no secrets between us."

"You know what I mean."

His expression sobered. "I do. And now that you're here, I hope you'll stay. I was just sitting here looking at my tree and wondering why I bothered to decorate it when there's no one to share it with."

"I was looking at my tree thinking the same thing," Virginia admitted.

She was lucky enough to have her children and grandchildren nearby. They had helped put up the tree, and many of the decorations were handmade keepsakes from elementary school or tiny family pictures in hanging frames. But Henry had almost no family in town. Had no one else seen his tree this season?

"Do you think maybe we should…get together and share a tree next year?" Henry asked. "So we don't have to sit in separate houses and look at our trees all alone."

She grinned at him. "I'd have to see what yours looks like first, and then maybe I could be convinced."

"Right this way."

"Wait," she said. "Let me grab something from my car. It's an early Christmas gift."

Virginia retrieved the wrapped sweater from the back seat of her car while Henry stood in his front door, waiting.

"You can open it now or tuck it under your tree," she said, handing him the package.

Virginia unzipped her winter coat and Henry put it on a hook inside the front door. She kicked off her boots and left them on the rug by the front door. Henry waited and then guided her into his living room, where a tall evergreen stood in front of a wide picture window. White lights circled the tree, but there were only a dozen red bulbs and another dozen miniature airplanes filling in the rest of the space.

"I know," he said. "It looks pretty sparse. I never had a real tree because I was always up in the air. Somehow, I thought one box of bulbs would go a lot farther than it did."

"I like the airplanes," Virginia commented.

"All gifts from family and coworkers. I was pretty excited to finally use them."

"I have carousel horses on mine. They were also gifts from people over the years because everyone knows I love the painted ponies."

Henry put the gift under the tree and then sat on the couch and pulled Virginia down next to him. He put an arm around her and she turned into his embrace to kiss him.

"When I came over here, this is exactly what I hoped would happen," Virginia said.

An oven timer in the kitchen rang loudly.

"I didn't plan on that," she joked.

"Dinner," Henry said. He touched his forehead to hers and kept his arm around her. "There's plenty for two if you like macaroni and cheese."

"I love it."

"I bought it frozen and just heated it up, so I can't take credit or blame for the quality."

"That's my favorite kind of cooking."

Henry offered Virginia a hand and they went into the kitchen. She waited while he slid the casserole dish out of the oven.

After turning Henry down for a real date a month and a half earlier, was it too late to ask for another chance? Everything about his verbal and body language told her to go ahead. She was the only person standing in her way.

"After dinner," she began. Henry's head snapped up and he parked the casserole dish on the counter and turned to face her. "Could I take you up on that offer of a glass of wine downtown?" she asked. "I love walking around and seeing the decorated windows and Christmas lights."

"And seeing Starlight Point from across the bay," he added.

"Especially that. I'm glad we're leaving the coaster lights on all winter this year. It makes the long, dark nights a lot more cheerful."

"You're making my winter more cheerful already."

"If we team up, we'll survive the cold to run the sand castle contest next summer and do battle with pumpkin eating squirrels next fall."

Henry smiled at her. "Next year, do you think there will be room on your tree for both airplanes and carousel horses?"

"That's why I'm here," she said.

Henry peeled off his oven mitts and put his warm hands on Virginia's cheeks. "I'd be happy to skip dinner and get straight to the wine, walking and whatever else you have in mind."

"There's plenty of time," Virginia said. "We've waited all summer. And I'd hate to miss out on the food. It'll help keep us warm."

Henry kissed her and Virginia knew she would have no trouble staying warm, no matter how hard the wind blew across the bay.

CHAPTER TWENTY-THREE

"LET ME HELP you with that," Nate said. "I have experience moving evergreen trees."

Alice stood aside while Nate hefted the potted tree. He followed her to one of the tall columns supporting the ballroom's roof. The elegant art deco room sparkled with Christmas cheer including evergreens, white lights, red tablecloths and glass hurricane lamps shielding white and gold candles on the tables.

"Lucky for us," Alice said, "we don't have to do all this work twice. Tonight's wedding is the last one before Christmas, and the bride and groom were happy to save money on decorations by using the ones we were buying anyway."

Nate picked up the next tree and followed Alice. He breathed heavily with the exertion of carrying the tree and with the excitement of what he wanted to say to her. He needed a chance to talk with her alone, but her usual staff of helpers, including Virginia and Henry—and Haley, who was home on college break—were all around asking for Alice's input and instructions on the decor and setup.

"About the dance," Nate said as he put down the tree and watched her wind lights around it. "I wanted to ask you—"

"I'm sure you received an invitation," Alice said, cutting him off. "All the year-round employees did. I hear it's quite a party."

Nate tipped his head and grinned at her. "Aren't you the one who sent the invitations out?"

"Yes."

"So you know I got one, and you know it says I can bring a guest."

"June and I did them together," Alice said. She avoided looking at him as she fussed excessively with a red ribbon on the tree. "June loves Christmas. A few years ago, her wedding merged with the employee holiday dance because all the year-round employees would have been invited anyway."

"That's really nice, but—"

Why was she avoiding talking to him? She

hadn't hesitated to practically dive into the marina to save him just a week ago.

"Over here, Henry," Alice called. She waved to Henry, who stood just inside the wide front doors of the ballroom with a tall Christmas tree over one shoulder.

"I've got the stand," Virginia said, appearing from behind a group of decorated potted evergreens on the other side of the room. She held a red metal tree stand over her head as if in victory. "Found it in storage before I came over."

"You two are a perfect combination," Alice said, smiling and shaking her head.

Nate noticed the look Virginia and Alice exchanged. It was the kind of look that suggested they both knew something or had already worked something out. He leaned down and whispered, "What's going on with those two?" His cheek brushed her hair and sent fire down his neck. He had to talk to her before he lost his mind or his nerve.

"You heard me," she said. "They make a good combination. I thought that was obvious all summer and fall." She didn't move away from him, which was a good sign.

Nate took Alice's arm and gently pulled her

behind a column. She didn't resist, instead tipping her head up and giving him her attention. How should he begin? "Can we talk?" *Very original.*

Alice swiped back a strand of auburn hair and tucked it into her ponytail. "Okay," she said.

"Here?" Nate wanted an opportunity to talk with her without anyone listening. What he had to say was so important he'd spent three days thinking of how he would say it. Would he get it right if he had to blurt it out in a roomful of people decorating for a wedding?

Alice shrugged. "It's snowing outside, and I need to make sure this gets done in the next hour or so. Could you tell me what's on your mind right now? I promise to give you my full attention."

He felt as if he was at the car dealership and the service manager was assuring him they were working diligently to get his oil changed. He wanted far more than her attention, especially with too many ears around.

As if it were an early gift, Christmas music started playing and filled the acoustically perfect ballroom with its rich sound. It created a cheerful wall of privacy around them. *Thank you, whoever put on the music.*

"I have a lot on my mind," he said. He took her hand. "First of all, thank you for saving my life."

Alice laughed nervously and picked evergreen needles out of her sweater's sleeve. "I didn't save your life. Your father is the one who hauled you onto the dock."

"You helped."

"I tried. You can't believe how happy I was to reach into the water and find my red scarf. Especially because you were attached to it."

"I never really believed I would die, but when I broke through the surface and saw you, I felt as if everything would be okay."

She flushed red. "You give me far too much credit."

"I'm telling the truth, and I'm not the only person who noticed it."

"I would have tried to save anyone."

"Am I just anyone to you?"

Alice shook her head and her eyes shone. Nate felt emotion welling up inside him, but he didn't try to fight it for the first time in years. He didn't know what to do next.

She studied his face as if she were at an

art exhibit and she was looking for clues in a painting. Under her scrutiny, he did the one thing that had always saved him. He struggled for a neutral expression and tried to smile as if he had everything under control.

Alice frowned.

The Christmas music switched from a cheerful vocal tune to an orchestral waltz. He wanted to dance with Alice, to have her all to himself in his arms. Was it possible for them to start over?

"You're not just anyone to me," she said. "I never wanted to hurt you." She breathed in and out slowly. "In fact, the reason I walked away from our wedding and our marriage was because I loved you...too much."

Nate felt as if he'd been punched. How could she love him too much and not marry him?

"I know you won't understand, at least I didn't think you would at the time."

"Why wouldn't I?" he asked.

"I didn't think you knew what it felt like to love someone so much it hurt. Our relationship was...disproportional. I felt I was giving you everything, but you were holding back. I tried to fool myself for a long time, thinking it would change as we got closer to the wedding."

Nate shook his head, his mouth open and his throat tight. "You're wrong."

"I didn't think so at the time. I loved you too much to marry you when I wasn't sure you loved me. It would have broken my heart on our wedding day and every day of our marriage after that."

"How can you think that I didn't love you? I asked you to marry me. I said I loved you. What else was I supposed to do?"

Tears spilled down her cheeks. She put a hand on his arm and looked genuinely sorry for him. "Every time you said I love you, you said it as if you were balancing a piece of glass or waiting for something to careen out of control."

"I meant it."

"I'm sorry, Nate. At the time, I couldn't marry someone who said I love you *cautiously*."

Nate had intended to open his heart to Alice, finally. After his breakdown with his father and his sister, he knew what he needed to do, even though it seemed pointless now.

He pulled an old newspaper clipping from his pocket and crushed it into Alice's hand.

She gave him a puzzled look and unfolded the delicate paper. "Is this you?" she asked at first. Nate didn't answer. Alice was reading the caption below the picture that revealed him as an object of pity, a poster child for what drunk drivers can do to a family. To a child. She held the photo in her hand and looked from it to Nate and back again.

He suspected his expression matched the sorrow of the child in the picture, himself fifteen years ago, knowing he'd lost something irreplaceable. He was exposing his vulnerability again, and he was afraid it wouldn't do any good. It hadn't brought back his mother when he'd cried for her at her funeral. And trying to show Alice his feelings now wasn't going to bring her back. He was afraid she wouldn't believe him if he said *I love you*.

"I never saw this picture," Alice said. "I knew what happened, of course, but I didn't read the paper when I was twelve. I'm sorry. Has this picture been haunting you all these years?"

Nate paused, hoping to find the words to

explain. "I felt humiliated every time the newspaper ran that picture in their campaign against drunken driving. It was a year-long effort to raise awareness in the area, spearheaded by my uncle, the police officer."

Alice slid into Nate's arms and hugged him. It was a promising sign that she wasn't walking away. They were behind a tall set of evergreens and practically alone. "Did he know how it made you feel to see that picture?" she asked, her words muffled against his chest.

Nate shook his head and his chin brushed her hair. He couldn't trust his voice to speak. Of course his uncle didn't know, and talking about his feelings with him would have been impossible. Nate's father would have stopped the ad campaign if he had known how Nate felt, but Nate had been afraid to add to his dad's grief by bringing up the subject.

Alice rubbed his back with one hand and put her palm on his cheek. He wanted to pull her close and kiss her. Would it still be as sweet as it was years ago? Being with her had made him almost forget the pain of his early teenage years. He'd taken a risk with his heart, and he believed he'd given her everything he had.

But now he knew she hadn't thought so, and then she'd left him, too.

He controlled his expression and squared his shoulders. "It was a long time ago. I just thought I would show you this picture because we were cleaning out some old stuff from my dad's attic." He sounded as if he was explaining to the lady at the thrift store why he was donating some old shoes he didn't need anymore. His father was right. Nate was so afraid of exposing his feelings that he couldn't convince the woman standing in front of him that he loved her.

Her face went from sympathetic to disappointed at his matter-of-fact tone. "I see," she said, tears shining in her eyes. "Thank you for sharing that picture with me." She swallowed and waited.

What should he say?

"But I should get back to work on these decorations," Alice said.

He nodded, too afraid to go one more step and say what was in his heart. Alice turned and walked away among the twinkling lights and music.

THE RIDE IN the open golf cart was short but brutally cold. Gloria drove, Virginia sat in the front seat, and Alice rode in the back seat with the wedding gown draped over her lap and wrapped in layers of plastic.

With the bridal gown in her arms, she thought of her own gown and wedding. Her mother had sold her dress the previous day and presented Alice with a nice check from the shop. Alice had no intention of cashing the check. She would hand it right back to her parents in a few more weeks when she'd finally put aside the total amount they had spent on her wedding. Paying them back would be a perfect way to celebrate the new year.

The gown was gone, but the groom was still in her life. Her conversation with Nate only hours earlier had left her with an empty sinking feeling. He'd been so sincere… Had he really loved her and she had misjudged him? And that picture. No wonder he never wanted to be caught off guard by his emotions. At the most vulnerable time in his life, someone had snapped a picture and used it for over a year. Despite the good intentions of his uncle and the local newspaper, Nate's ability to show his feelings had been powerfully supplanted by his desire to appear fine, no matter what. No doubt he considered it safer.

If we'd only talked about it years ago...

"Slow down, Gloria," Virginia said. "I want to live to see this wedding."

"Won't be a wedding," Gloria said as she slid around a corner and whooshed to a stop in front of the wardrobe department at Starlight Point. "Not unless I get a new zipper in that dress in the next twenty minutes."

Alice handed over the dress to Virginia as she climbed out and the three of them froze outside the door while Gloria fumbled with her keys. "Supposed to have the winter off, but you keep finding more stuff for me to do," she muttered. "Halloween costumes, Santa costumes and now emergency wedding repairs."

Gloria shoved open the door and flipped on the lights while Virginia and Alice carried the long, awkwardly wrapped package to a broad sewing table. They unwrapped the gown and laid it out for the head seamstress to work her magic. Gloria pulled open drawers and sorted through them until she held up a long ivory zipper. "Hallelujah. It's the right kind. Can't believe I had one."

"We've been friends for thirty years," Virginia told Gloria as she pulled up a chair next to her at the industrial sewing machine. "So I can definitely believe you had one. You've been keeping this place put together for years. What would we do without you?"

"I'll probably just keep coming back until you find my skeleton sitting at this machine with a measuring tape draped around my neck and a pincushion attached to my wrist."

Alice wandered around the shop while Gloria carefully ripped out the tiny stitches that held the gown's zipper. She was too nervous to sit down and too restless to stop pacing.

"It'll be fine," Gloria told Alice on her third pass by the sewing machine. "Don't think this is my first emergency, and it sure won't be the last."

Alice smiled. "I know. I'm not nervous about the dress. We're lucky to have a professional on staff, and if the wedding is ten minutes late, I don't think it will lead to cold feet or second thoughts."

Gloria laughed. "People are bound to get those anyway. I remember thinking I was making the biggest mistake of my life when I looked down the aisle and saw that skinny boy I'd agreed to marry."

"And what happened?"

Gloria shrugged. "He grew on me." She pulled the broken zipper out of the gown and clipped all the threads. Stuffing her mouth with pins, she began to line up the new zipper and fix it in place.

Virginia spun in her chair. "Tell me about the couple getting married today," she told Alice.

"High school sweethearts. I actually knew them because they were just one class behind me and Nate in school."

"You and Nate?"

Alice nodded. She couldn't believe she had included him in the conversation, but when she thought about that time in her life, Nate was always right there in her memories.

"We knew each other in high school."

Virginia raised an eyebrow. "To say the least."

"Yes," Alice admitted. "Anyway, today's bride and groom dated in high school, split up in college and got back together last year."

"Happy ending," Gloria muttered through the pins.

"I hope so."

"And what are you going to do about Nate?" Virginia asked.

Alice sucked in a breath and noticed Gloria's head swing in her direction. She knew people were talking about the fact they were once together. There were very few secrets in a place as small and family-oriented as Starlight Point. And Alice saw no reason to conceal it any longer. She had, for his sake. But now...

"It's been five years since I ruined our rehearsal dinner by announcing I wasn't going through with the wedding."

"You were young," Virginia said sympathetically. "Although I've discovered recently that old age doesn't protect you from letting your heart lead you on a wild ride."

"I want to hear more about that in a minute," Gloria said as she took the last pin from between her teeth.

"It wasn't just being twenty-two," Alice protested. "I was a very wise twenty-two."

Gloria and Virginia both laughed.

"Okay, fine," Alice said, laughing, too. "I thought I was very grown up. And I don't regret my decision. I was right to say no at the time."

Gloria sighed and turned her attention to the zipper in the gown that would be worn by a bride who hadn't changed her mind.

Henry breezed through the door and stamped snow off his boots. A cold wind swirled through the wardrobe shop.

"I came over to see if I could help."

"Can you sew?" Gloria asked.

"I'm more muscle and moral support."

"Come back in May. I can use you then," Gloria said. "I have more than enough help right now."

"In that case, can I borrow one of your helpers?" he asked, looking straight at Virginia. "I need some help with an important question."

Even though Alice didn't know exactly what the question was, she felt the thrill in Henry's voice and noticed the tremor in Virginia's lip. Raw emotion and joy showed on both their faces. Equally. Neither of them was holding back.

That was what Alice wanted from Nate, and what he'd been unable to give her when she needed it most.

CHAPTER TWENTY-FOUR

"A TOAST," JACK SAID, popping the cork on a bottle of champagne. "To *not* wearing matching sweaters for this picture."

"I'll drink to that," Evie said.

Nate waited for instructions, camera dangling from his neck. He was already dressed for the employee Christmas party, which would begin in only half an hour. Not in a holiday mood, he still struggled with Alice's words from the day before.

He'd been angry and defensive at first, but then he replayed his memories of those years they dated and were engaged. The caution she had accused him of using...maybe she was right. Ever since his mother was there one moment and gone the next, he confused loving someone with fearing they would leave.

When Alice had left him, it only confirmed and deepened that feeling.

"If I hear any complaining about taking

a family Christmas photo, I will personally knit you all a matching sweater for next year," Virginia announced, hand on hip.

June shoulder-hugged her. "You don't know how to knit, Mom."

"I'm never too old to try something new."

Nate wondered if Henry would be Virginia's date for the party. He was lingering just down the hall, nervously picking at the knot in his green-and-red-striped tie. Nate had seen him when he went to his office to pick up the high-quality camera he used for updating the company blog and website.

A few minutes later, the entire Hamilton family assembled in front of the large tree in the corporate office lobby. They were all dressed for the holiday party. Nate had already seen some early guests arriving. Ladies wore cocktail dresses with a little sparkle. Men wore suits with fun Christmas ties that lit up or played music. Children wore holiday dresses and suits.

"This is the first whole group photo we've had done in years," Virginia said. "And our family has grown so much. We have to make sure to take one every year."

"Thanks for helping us out," Jack told Nate as he handed him a glass of champagne.

"No trouble for me—I don't have to be in it," Nate said. Which was a good thing because he didn't think he could even fake a smile.

"Gather in front of the tree," Evie directed. "Tall people in the back."

Everyone laughed. Jack and his best friend, Mel, were both over six foot three, and June and Evie neared the six-foot mark. Looking at the next generation, Nate imagined they would be tall, too. What a nice family. So happy, despite losing someone tragically just five years ago. He knew what it was like to lose someone. Did he know what it was like to heal and be whole again?

While Nate watched the family assemble in front of the tree, he noticed Henry standing in the doorway that led to the hallway of offices. He seemed to be waiting.

Virginia lined up her children and grandchildren, standing in front of them as if conducting an orchestra. When she had them assembled, she gestured to Henry to come over.

She took Henry's hand in front of her family. Everyone waited and Nate felt the tension in the room. He wanted to fade into the woodwork, but he'd been invited, asked to be there.

"I may not learn to knit," Virginia said, "but I have learned something new lately. When Ford passed away, I didn't think there could ever be room in my heart for someone else. And for a long time, there wasn't. Maybe it's all the weddings I've helped with this year. Every time I see the joy on the faces of the bride and groom and their families, it reminds me that life goes on."

Evie and June started crying. Mel dug tissues from the pocket of his coat and handed one to his wife and sister-in-law.

"When my longtime friend got married last month, I thought at first it was a big mistake. But when I asked myself why—more specifically when Alice Birmingham asked me why I objected—I couldn't think of a single good reason."

Nate wished Alice couldn't think of any reasons she shouldn't be with him.

"I realized I was afraid of my own feelings," Virginia continued. "I loved your father with all my heart, and I was afraid if I opened my heart to someone else, Ford would fade away. But he can never fade away. He's everywhere at Starlight Point. In the swinging cable cars and the carousel music. And in all of us. But I don't think he'd mind if I shared that carousel music with someone new who came into my life like a roller coaster."

Henry put an arm around Virginia and kissed her cheek.

Virginia smiled. "I love Henry, and I hope you can all accept that it's time for me to love again." She paused and looked at Henry. "Do you want to tell them or should I?"

Henry straightened his tie and faced the entire family. *He is one brave man.* "Yesterday afternoon, I asked Virginia to marry me."

"And I said yes!" she cried.

Nate started snapping pictures as Jack shook hands with Henry and then pulled him into a hug. Mel and Scott stepped forward and welcomed Henry with handshakes after June, Evie and Augusta had hugged him and cried on his suit.

Nate zoomed in and took pictures of the children. He doubted they understood what a milestone moment it was for the Hamilton family, but they certainly picked up on the joy. He saw it in their shining faces.

He imagined an album filled with candid photos of this night plus one large group photo. He glanced at his watch. The Christmas party was in only fifteen minutes, and he still hadn't found a way to convince Alice he was ready to love someone with all his heart.

When Evie and Virginia got the group reassembled in front of the tree, Nate felt a wash of relief. He could get the picture and make his way to the dance. Maybe he could get a moment alone with Alice before the party got going.

"One, two, three," he counted, framing the shot to include the entire Hamilton family with the Christmas tree behind them. Their faces said everything. Joy, excitement, happiness, a new beginning for them. He took three pictures, just to make certain he got a good one, and on the third picture, something clicked into place for him.

He remembered the video Henry had taken of him skating with Alice. The look of pure wonder and joy on his own face when he'd struggled to his feet and looked down at Alice. That was the moment he knew he loved her, still and again, but he'd never been brave enough to show it to anyone. It was raw, vulnerable and showed what was in his heart. There was one person who had to see it.

CHAPTER TWENTY-FIVE

"WHAT DID YOU do to my mother?" June asked as she joined Alice behind the reception table. "The entire family holds you responsible for her happiness."

Alice turned, afraid she'd meddled in the wrong romance. She opened her mouth to apologize, but June was smiling.

"She just announced her engagement to Henry as we were trying to take a giant family photo in front of the office tree. I'm sure we'll all look tearstained in the picture."

"But happy," Alice said. Her heart swelled with joy for Virginia and Henry.

"Very. Evie and I have been trying to tell her to join a singles group for the past year, but I guess it took meeting the right guy and seeing her friend take a chance on a second marriage."

"I'm glad for her."

June nodded. "I told you before that I'm a

sucker for a second-chance romance. Mel and I wouldn't be married now if I hadn't had the wisdom to pursue him."

"Is that how it happened?"

"Not exactly. I tried running, but not too fast. I gave him a fighting chance to catch me."

Alice smiled.

"And now, I'm on a mission," June said. "I've been asked to make sure you see something." She took Alice by the shoulders and turned her so she could see the screen behind them.

Puzzled, Alice looked at the giant video screen. She saw herself ice skating in a green velvet jacket and a long green skirt. Of course! It was the promotional video. Her spirits lifted for the first time since she'd shut down Nate's attempt to talk to her the day before. She always felt free and happy moving swiftly across the ice, and she vividly remembered that morning a month ago when she'd tried out the temporary rink in the parking lot. Other people stopped to watch the video of her skating, but then the shot cut to Nate wobbling precariously on his borrowed skates.

Bystanders chuckled and a small crowd gathered to watch the screen.

On the big screen, she watched herself take his hand and lead him around the ice, holding him tight before he fell. Tears collected in her eyes as she remembered the moment and how warm his fingers had felt through her gloves.

As she watched the screen with tears blurring her vision, she saw Nate fall. She knew what happened next, knew she would see herself help him to his feet. Henry had stood across the rink with the camera, and her back was to him. She saw her red hair contrast with the green jacket, and then Nate's face appeared in the frame over her shoulder.

Her heart nearly stopped when she saw the expression on his face. *It was the look.* The look she often saw grooms give their brides before they walked down the aisle. Absolute helplessness in the face of true love. For Nate, total and complete vulnerability and honesty.

"Wonder-eyes," June whispered.

She'd seen parts of this video before. There were clips of it on the company website. But she'd never seen this part, and she knew exactly why. Not many people were brave enough to open their hearts for others to see. The movie stopped, frozen with the final image of her back, Nate's dumbfounded expression, and the tall roller coasters of Starlight Point behind them.

Nate stepped out from behind the screen. He wore a black suit with a Christmas green tie. "I couldn't find the words to tell you, so I had to show you."

Alice waited, hoping the video meant what she believed it did. She wanted to run to him and throw herself into his arms, but she knew he had to be the one to come to her.

"When I first watched the footage Henry shot, I cringed at my lack of talent compared to your grace. And then when I saw that," he said, pointing to the screen, "I thought I would never let anyone watch it. I was afraid to let down my guard and let people see straight into my heart."

Alice couldn't help herself. She stepped toward him, close enough to touch his silk tie.

"But you did."

"I'm not afraid anymore," Nate said, slipping an arm around Alice. "The only thing I'm afraid of is losing you for the second time."

"I love you, Nate. I never stopped."

"I love you, too, and I'm not saying that cautiously. I love you with dangerous, wild, and totally reckless hope for our future."

The crowd assembled for the party broke into spontaneous laughter, and Nate didn't flinch at the sudden attention.

Alice laughed and kissed him, relishing the feel of his lips that were so familiar and finally hers for good. She pointed to his face on the screen, the large image exposed to the entire room. "I know."

EPILOGUE

NATE LEANED OVER and whispered in Alice's ear. "Nice job planning this wedding."

Alice smiled, enjoying his lips brushing her ear and sending out sensations of excitement and happiness. "It's the wedding of the year."

Nate wrapped an arm around Alice as they waited for the ceremony to begin. The Starlight Point ferry pulled away from the dock in downtown Bayside and sounded its horn. It was the first weekend in May, and the park was slated to open in only seven days for what they hoped would be a blockbuster season.

"This is fun, and they got lucky with the weather," Nate said. The spring breeze had a little chill, but the sun shone on the bay and the water was calm.

"June, Evie and I had a backup plan," Alice

said, "but it wouldn't have been as much fun as this."

All the guests—forty of them—had been instructed to park downtown and get on the one o'clock ferry. Ken, their long-serving captain, who'd retired from the navy, would chart a course around the Starlight Point peninsula while the ceremony took place. The ferry would then dock at the Starlight Point Marina for an afternoon reception of cake and champagne at the marina restaurant.

"Here they come," Alice said. All the guests turned toward the back of the boat, where Virginia and Henry were walking down the aisle, arm in arm. They touched each bench seat on their way, for balance, Alice thought, and also to connect with their guests.

Every person invited was special to the engaged couple, their families and Starlight Point.

The ferry slowed to a crawl and rocked almost imperceptibly as the bride and groom stood before their guests. Henry wrapped an arm around Virginia's waist and held her tight. He wore a black suit with a crisp blue tie. Virginia wore an ivory dress with a matching jacket. The minister stepped forward and asked the bride and groom to face each other for the reading of the vows. Alice waited and held her breath.

"Is that the look?" Nate whispered to Alice as Henry turned to Virginia and smiled.

"Wonder-eyes," she whispered back. "I knew we'd see it today."

While the sunshine sparkled on the blue water, Virginia and Henry pledged their love and faithfulness to each other. Jack and Augusta, pregnant with a son due later in the summer, sat in the front row with their daughter, Nora. June and Mel joined them with Ross and Abigail, who wore a pink dress matching her cousin Nora's. Evie cradled her baby boy, named after his grandfather Ford, with Scott at her side. The other guests were mostly full-time employees of Starlight Point with some of Virginia and Henry's friends in the mix. Henry's pilot friends from his years with the airline had come. Virginia's friend Judy and her new husband, Mike, sat across from Alice and Nate.

Second chances, Alice thought.

"Are we next?" Nate asked Alice as Virginia and Henry kissed.

"I'd kiss you anytime."

He smiled. "You know what I mean. Our wedding. I'm waiting for you to name the date."

Alice's heart raced. She and Nate had talked about getting married and were officially engaged—again. She toyed with the band of her diamond ring while she considered her answer.

"My sister is getting married in June," she said.

"And?"

"And we're really busy in the summer with our jobs at the Point."

Alice watched the hired waiters fill champagne flutes for a toast as the ferry approached Starlight Point. She waited for them to get to her row of seats while she imagined her wedding to Nate for the hundredth time.

"I'm not a wedding planner," Nate said, clinking his glass to hers, "but I do have a great idea for ours."

They were interrupted by a toast from Jack in honor of his mother's wedding. Wisely, Jack kept it short, and everyone cheered and toasted the new couple.

"The train," Nate said. "We'll just have to

be careful with the guest list to make sure no one fights and jumps off."

Alice laughed. "How about while ice skating this Christmas? I think we'll make the rink twice as large this year based on last year's response."

"I'll marry you anywhere and anytime," Nate said.

She closed her eyes and kissed him. The boat rocked gently and she tasted champagne and sweetness.

"This summer," she said. "On the beach in front of the Lake Breeze Hotel. We'll have a reception in the rotunda. I didn't tell you, but I did pencil in two possible dates with the wedding planner at Starlight Point. I have connections."

Nate smiled. "I'll practice my wonder-eyes."

She laughed. "You don't have to. You're doing it perfectly right now."

The Starlight Point ferry rounded the tip of the peninsula, champagne flowed, and all the wedding guests looked forward to wedding cake and a summer of carefree days.

* * * * *

Get 2 Free Books,
Plus 2 Free Gifts—
just for trying the Reader Service!

Love Inspired®

HOME on the RANCH

YES! Please send me the **Home on the Ranch Collection** in Larger Print. This collection begins with 3 FREE books and 2 FREE gifts in the first shipment. Along with my 3 free books, I'll also get the next 4 books from the Home on the Ranch Collection, in LARGER PRINT, which I may either return and owe nothing, or keep for the low price of $5.24 U.S./ $5.89 CDN each plus $2.99 for shipping and handling per shipment*. If I decide to continue, about once a month for 8 months I will get 6 or 7 more books, but will only need to pay for 4. That means 2 or 3 books in every shipment will be FREE! If I decide to keep the entire collection, I'll have paid for only 32 books because 19 books are FREE! I understand that accepting the 3 free books and gifts places me under no obligation to buy anything. I can always return a shipment and cancel at any time. My free books and gifts are mine to keep no matter what I decide.

268 HCN 3760 468 HCN 3760

Name	(PLEASE PRINT)	
Address		Apt. #
City	State/Prov.	Zip/Postal Code

Signature (if under 18, a parent or guardian must sign)

Mail to the **Reader Service:**

IN U.S.A.: P.O. Box 1867, Buffalo, NY. 14240-1867
IN CANADA: P.O. Box 609, Fort Erie, Ontario L2A 5X3

* Terms and prices subject to change without notice. Prices do not include applicable taxes. Sales tax applicable in NY. Canadian residents will be charged applicable taxes. This offer is limited to one order per household. All orders subject to approval. Credit or debit balances in a customer's account(s) may be offset by any other outstanding balance owed by or to the customer. Please allow 3 to 4 weeks for delivery. Offer available while quantities last. Offer not available to Quebec residents.

Get 2 Free Books,
Plus 2 Free Gifts –

just for trying the *Reader Service!*

Get 2 Free Books,
Plus 2 Free Gifts—
just for trying the
Reader Service!

❤ HARLEQUIN®

SPECIAL EDITION

READERSERVICE.COM

Manage your account online!

- Review your order history
- Manage your payments
- Update your address

> ### We've designed the Reader Service website just for you.

Enjoy all the features!

- Discover new series available to you, and read excerpts from any series.
- Respond to mailings and special monthly offers.
- Browse the Bonus Bucks catalog and online-only exculsives.
- Share your feedback.

Visit us at:

ReaderService.com